Best Books for

WINNING

WINNING

by Robin F. Brancato

ALFRED A. KNOPF NEW YORK

The characters in this novel are
purely fictional. Any resemblance
between them and persons living or
dead is unintentional and
coincidental.

This is a Borzoi Book published by Alfred A. Knopf, Inc.

Copyright © 1977 by Robin F. Brancato
All rights reserved under International and Pan-American Copyright
Conventions. Published in the United States by Alfred A. Knopf, Inc.,
New York, and simultaneously in Canada by Random House of Canada
Limited, Toronto. Distributed by Random House, Inc., New York.
Manufactured in the United States of America

Library of Congress Cataloging in Publication Data
Brancato, Robin. Winning.
Summary: Paralyzed as a result of a football accident, a high school
student struggles to accept the reality of his condition and the effect
it will have on his friendships and his future.
[1. Physically handicapped—Fiction] I. Title.
PZ7.B73586Wi   [Fic]   77-5632
ISBN 0-394-83581-6
10 9 8 7 6 5 4 3 2

For John,
with love

acknowledgments

I would like to thank the many people whose willingness to give me time and information made *Winning* possible. From the conception of the idea to the completion of the novel, I have been overwhelmed by the generosity of both patients and medical professionals.

I would like to extend my appreciation first to the entire staff and the patients of the Kessler Institute for Rehabilitation, West Orange, New Jersey, and in particular to Mr. William Page, executive director; Dr. Richard Sullivan, medical director; and Mr. James Tucker, director of the physical therapy department.

I would also like to thank the individuals who granted me personal interviews and who, in some cases, gave me criticism of the manuscript: Dr. Gordon Engler, Mr. Robert Grant, R.P.T., Fran and Mike LoRusso, Dr. Eric Naftchi, Dr. Frank Padrone, Mr. James Pasciuti, Dr. Kristjan T. Ragnarsson, Francisco Santillana, and Bill Scott.

In addition, I wish to express thanks to Elaine Lugovoy, Suzanne Schecter, and Natalie Snyder for helping me obtain background reading material, to Maria Costa for providing me with photographs, and to the following people whose advice and encouragement were critical to the completion of my work: Barbara Cunningham, Judy Liebman, Libby Machol, Charles R. Marsh, Dr. Eric Simon, Isabel Wolfson, and Laura Woodworth.

Finally, I thank my husband John for his unflagging interest and essential constructive criticism.

Robin F. Brancato

April 1977

WINNING

chapter 1

Gary, facedown, looked through the small opening in his canvas bed at the patch of floor that he already knew by heart.

"Gary, your friends from the high school are here. Your mother's going to bring them in as soon as we turn you."

Visitors—great. About time for a switch, too, after two solid hours lying on his stomach.

Now he could see the feet of the nurse, Sister Marie, who in a minute would be calling the orderly to help her flip him over on his Stryker frame. There must be a better way to turn a guy who couldn't move by himself, to keep him from getting bedsores. A way that wouldn't scare the hell out of a person the way the Stryker did. It wasn't something you got used to, not even after every two hours, twelve times a day for thirteen days.

All systems were being okayed now. Sister Marie was checking out the steel tongs planted in his skull that kept him from turning his head. Tongs with a thirty-five-pound weight attached were hotshot Dr. Kimball's idea of how to straighten out a spinal column. Bad enough to be down and out—did they have to put you on the rack? Thirteen days in the hospital, turns twelve times a day. Let's see . . . that'd be one hundred fifty-six flips. He could tell Sister Marie how to do it by now. O.K., Sister, lift the top half of the frame that looks like a stretcher. Lay it on my back and clamp it to the stretcher underneath me. Great. The bologna in a sandwich, that's what he felt like.

"I'll be right back, Gary," Sister Marie said. "I'm going to get the orderly."

Hurry, Gary thought. Get this over with. Better to be anywhere than here in this contraption. Where would he go if he could choose? Back to exactly two weeks ago, maybe. Opening-game pep rally in the gym during the last period. The team, in their too-big mesh jerseys, lined up, shuffling and embarrassed as Coach Lausch introduced them one by one. "At middle linebacker this year," Buck Lausch had announced, "a senior with enough experience and spirit for a whole team—Gary Madden!" And Gary had stepped forward, eyes lowered the way the kids expected you to look, and had kept his face solemn while they clapped and cheered and spelled out his name. And after the rally, on his way to the fieldhouse for Buck's psych session, Diane in her blue flag bearer's uniform had met him. They had stood together under the hidden stairway near the home ec room . . .

Footsteps now, confusion. His mother's voice. A hand on his shoulder.

"Ready, Gary?" Sister Marie asked.

Gary closed his eyes. *Help, the rack! No, not the rack!* "Yeah, I'm ready," he said. Being on the frame these two weeks had made him remember a fantasy he used to act out as a little kid in bed at night: Fiendish madmen were torturing him, trying to make him give up the key to the secret code, but he wouldn't break down. Not a whimper, either. Not him. He had taken to playing the same game now sometimes.

He felt a jolt. What if the clamps gave and he got dumped, the weight pulling crazily on his skull? The bed stopped turning. Gary, on his back, saw the cream-colored ceiling and then the face of his mother, who was standing above him. Sister Marie unfastened the top half of the frame, lifted it off him.

"Everything all right?" she asked.

"Just fine," Gary's mother said. "Right, Gary?"

"Yeah." As Sister Marie went out, he took in everything in his new line of vision—as much as he could see with a head stuck, like an ice cube, in tongs. The one wall, where his get-well cards and newspaper clippings and his New Bridge High School pennant were taped up. The story had been in all the papers: *Local Athlete Hospitalized as Lions Score Victory.* They were doing a series now because of him—*Is High School Football Safe Enough?* Up there on the other wall he could see the crucifix, standard equipment for St. Agnes Hospital, where they'd brought him because it was nearest; and beyond that, the top half of the window. Under the window was an area he couldn't see. They were bringing him a roommate later today to fill that spot. Gray light was coming in the window now. A dreary, drizzly fall day . . . it was Friday, wasn't it? School must be over if visitors were here.

"Who's out there, Ma?" he asked. *Say Diane.*

His mother was wiping his forehead, lifting one of his arms and then the other and laying them across his stomach. "Your English teacher, Mrs. Treer, is here, and your friend Billy, and that other young man from the football team—"

"Jason? Jason Lovett?" He knew without asking. There was a certain overpolite tone she always used to refer to anybody black.

"Yes, Jason."

"That's all?"

"Diane's here, too. She said she'll wait until last."

"Good." Great. Double great. Maybe he'd see Diane alone for a change.

"Drink your water now," his mother said. She held the cup while he drank slowly through a bent straw.

Ridiculous to drink lying flat on your back. Keep going though, three quarts a day. Flush out those kidneys.

His mother took away the cup and smoothed his hair. Man, she was really looking beat. How come he hadn't noticed before? She must have just put on fresh lipstick, but it was too red and made her look old. Had she been getting old all along, or was it this mess that was knocking her out? She'd been with him practically around the clock since the beginning. Right away, in fact, when they'd carried him off the field on a board, he had heard her saying *Everything's going to be all right.* And in the ambulance she was there, and in that blur in the emergency room, when they were debating who to call, and what to do next, and asking him all the time *Can you move this? Can you feel that?* She had stayed for the first couple of nights in the Intensive Care Unit, and ever since then she'd been running here to help the nurses and to keep him company. His father had hung in, too, but somehow it was his mother's voice and face he remembered out of all the confusion.

"There," she said, smoothing his sheet, "now you're ready for company."

"Am I covered?" he whispered.

"Of course you're covered. Would I let you lie there in your bare skin?"

No, but he worried about it just the same. He'd even had a nightmare: There he was, running hurdles in front of a huge crowd, with only a towel wrapped around his middle, and some goofball had yanked off the towel. . . .

"I'll go tell your guests to come in, Gary." His mother went to the door. "Then I'm going to the ladies' room for a few minutes to freshen up."

Hurry, he thought. Billy, Jason, Treer. Then Diane. He'd had a bunch of visitors in the last week, ever since they'd let people in—the team, teachers, kids he didn't even know. At first it had been an ego trip having so many people come up. But after they'd seen him, some kids didn't know what to say. One group had ignored him, had just joked with one another as if it was a not-very-sad funeral and he was the dead guy. And the coaches were acting a little weird, too. Coach Hammer kept glancing away—so he wouldn't have to look at the tongs, maybe? Buck Lausch was too quiet. Did the coaches know something he didn't know? Fractured vertebrae and trauma to the spinal cord—that's what Dr. Kimball called his problem. Spinal cord not severed. Hope for the best. Kimball wouldn't lie, would he? His parents wouldn't lie. . . .

He heard voices at the door. What're ya gabbing about

out there, Ma? Let 'em come in! Was he only imagining that people were always talking about him? Here they were. First time Treer had been to see him.

"Hi, Gary, we've missed you in class."

"Hi," he said. Ms. Ann Treer. Preferred to be called *Mzzz*. Not bad-looking. Young. Long, dark hair. Tough as a teacher. Sort of a stiff, snobby type. Oh, yeah, husband killed last year in a car accident. All of the kids at school had talked about it.

"Hi, Gary," Billy said.

"Hi, Bill." Hey, buddy, don't look away. Been through a lot together, right? Don't worry. Everything's gonna be O.K.

"Hey, Gary." Jason edged closer. "How you feeling?"

"Not bad. You're getting taller every time I see you."

"Just depends on your point of view, man," Jason said. "Actually I shrank an inch since yesterday."

"The Incredible Shrinking Man," Gary said. "Ever see that flick?"

"Yeah," Jason nodded. "That's the dude ends up living in a dollhouse."

Silence. It was rough trying to look at all three of them. The nurses had promised to rig up a mirror tonight so he could see people better. "Did you all come together?" he asked.

"Yeah," Billy said. "Buck—I mean Mr. Lausch—let us off practice, and Ms. Treer offered us a ride."

Jason smiled. "Don't say you didn't ever do anything for us, Gary. You can picture what we're missing over there in the fieldhouse, right?"

"Yeah," Gary said. "Buck still big on Friday psyching sessions?"

"Voodoo, I call it," Jason laughed.

"Don't put it down," Billy said. The team's got to get psyched. The Cougars are really up for tomorrow, I hear."

Gary half listened. Billy was rattling on now about tomorrow. Tomorrow, when they were on the field, he'd still be lying here. And for five more games after that, probably. At first he figured he'd be back for the end of the season. Now—almost two weeks and not much change. Every morning when he first woke up he'd try his right arm, then his left. Then his legs. No movement below the shoulders. And no feeling. Only that same band of uncomfortableness around his chest and the dull heaviness down below. He'd gotten a few flickers of sensation on the insides of his arms when the resident pricked him with a pin, but no big improvement. *What's the story, Dr. Kimball?*

Spinal shock took awhile to wear off. That's what Kimball had told him twelve days ago. Now Kimball wasn't saying much when he came on rounds. He was cheerful, friendly. Was that supposed to mean everything would be O.K.?

"Hey, Gary, Buck's putting Putnam in at middle linebacker tomorrow," Billy said.

"Yeah, I know." Gary looked from Billy to Ms. Treer, caught her off guard. Don't get scared, Ms. Treer. Same old *B*-plus Gary Madden, row three, seat five, just temporarily out of order. "Interested in football, Ms. Treer?"

"Yes," she said, "as far as it's connected with the school. I don't like pro football."

"No?" Gary yawned.

"You go to the New Bridge games?" Billy asked her. "Have you seen us play?"

"No, not this year. I've been away a lot of weekends."

Lull in the conversation again. Gary watched her. Uptight for a teacher her age.

"I've brought you something, Gary," she said. "A book." Treer reached in her bag, held up a gift-wrapped package.

"Thanks," he said. Damn, he was still forgetting that he couldn't put his hand out and grab. In his mind he was moving the hand that lay across his gut.

"Have you been able to—have you felt like reading yet?" she asked, looking around for a place to put the gift.

"Mom's read to me a little," he said. "Letters, mostly. I can read with prism glasses, but somebody's got to hold up whatever I'm reading." Man, it was going to be rough catching up with all his schoolwork. He'd already missed a lot of classes.

"Who have you gotten letters from?" Ms. Treer asked.

"Oh, guys who played football, parents, little kids . . . everybody." Treer was straining to make conversation. At least she was trying. Billy and Jason were just standing there like clods. What were they, shy in front of a teacher?

"Here comes your mother," Jason said.

Good. Just in time. His mother liked to talk. Let her entertain Treer.

"How's everybody doing?" she asked, patting his shoulder.

"O.K." He yawned again.

"He's had a lot of visitors, hasn't he?" Treer asked.

"Oh, yes," his mother said. "People have been wonderful. From the minute it happened, people have been so wonderful. . . ."

Keep talking, Ma, keep talking. Better you than me. What was it she had just said? *From the minute it happened.*

Which minute? What had happened? So far, everybody had a version. What was his? Go back two Saturdays ago to the game against the Bears. A bum first half. Moran had screwed up that pass. Savino had got them a fifteen-yard penalty. And him, Madden the Masochist, beat from clobbering the Bears' Lionetti, play after play.

But half time had revived him. Buck Lausch, trying to make them angry, had gone with the usual rap: "You aren't *using* what you *got!*" Wally Hammer, slapping butts: "Winning is the second step—*wanting to win* is the first!" Jason, to him: "Football's a *job,* man. You're the only jock that *worked* first half." Well, he had gone and done it. He had used himself, wanted to win, worked. Hitting Jimmy Lionetti, he had felt a weird zing. No pain—just a zing. And he had been as surprised as anybody when he couldn't get up. Couldn't. Can't. And no feeling. Still none. "Ma!"

"Yes?"

"Water, Ma."

His mother, talking to Treer, measured water.

Billy bent over him. "I just came by to say hello, Gary. I'm gonna go now. I got to get back to the field house. Diane'll take my place. See you tomorrow after the game."

"O.K., Bill, thanks for coming."

"I'm going, too," Jason said. "Got an errand downtown. Buck told me I didn't have to come back. Stay cool, Gary." He rapped the frame with his fist. "Make sure they strap you tight on that funhouse ride. See you tomorrow."

"Hey, you guys"—Gary looked from one of them to the other—"tell the team . . . win."

"Sure," Billy said. "So long, Jason. So long, Gary. 'Bye, Mrs. Madden, Ms. Treer."

His mother and Treer were saying goodbye.

Jason paused, put his hand on Gary's shoulder. "I'd trade wins to see you on your feet, man."

"Thanks." Why was Jason looking at him such a long time?

"Hey," Jason said, shaking his head, "didn't mean to get so heavy. O.K., a quick one before I take off: What's hard-headed, got a long shaft, and bangs everything in sight?"

Gary smiled. "What?"

Jason waited a second. "A hammer, man. A Coach Wally Hammer!"

"Get outa here!"

" 'Bye, buddy."

"So long." O.K., Diane, it's your turn now, if my mother and Treer ever stop talking. Too bad circumstances are so lousy, Diane. No privacy. Bed—if you can call it that—too skinny even to sit on the edge of. Bottle of pee hanging there not very romantically. My pee. Watch for blood in it, they say. That's a bad sign. What's a good sign, Diane? Gimme one?

A rumble in the hall. "Diane?"

"Diane'll be here in a minute, Gary," his mother said, "as soon as they finish bringing in the other patient."

A clatter at the door. "Who is he?"

"A nice young man. Nineteen years old."

Nice young man. That would be his mother's code for somebody white. College kid, maybe. "What's he got? What's wrong with him?"

"He hurt his back."

"Broken?"

"Yes, he's had an operation. They've brought him here from another hospital."

The cart was rolling by the end of his frame. A roommate. That could be a big improvement. Somebody to talk to in those dead spaces when visitors left; another person here in the middle of the night.

Good. Things were looking up, actually. . . . He'd thought he felt a new twinge on his lower arm today. Only a matter of time. Meanwhile, relax. A lousy situation to be in, but it could have been worse. He was safe now. He'd pulled through. And hell, he was strong! Hardly been sick a day in his life. And he was getting the best care—everybody told him that. Sister Marie was practically living just to take care of his skin. Insurance pretty good, and people contributing toward the medical bills. Rotten deal, but may as well make the best of it. Probably the only time he'd ever be able to take it this easy. No homework. Automatic peeing machine! Fed with a spoon by his mother. Whispered to by Diane, who right this minute was on her way to him.

The orderlies were bustling around the new guy now.

"You've got a roommate, Gary," the orderly said. "This is Tom Frechette. Make sure you two guys stay out of trouble."

"O.K.," Gary said.

"*Trouble,*" a voice from the other side of the room mumbled, "hell, trouble's my middle name."

"I'll be leaving now," Treer was saying.

"Thanks for the book," Gary said. "So long."

"We're so glad you came, Mrs. Treer . . . it is *Mrs.*, isn't it?"

"*Ms.*, Ma."

"Ann," Treer told her.

"Oh, yes. Well, let me see you to the door," his mother said. "And please come again."

Yeah, Gary thought, but not too soon. Got another visitor now. Where was she?

"Hi, Gary."

Oh, man. She was leaning over the frame. Her hair was brushing against his cheek. "Hi, Diane. . . ." Clean. Smelling of lemons. Please let his mother have a long farewell with Treer.

"I wanted to be last," Diane whispered, touching her forehead to his. "Sorry I kept you waiting."

"That's O.K.," he said. "It was worth it."

chapter 2

Ann Treer walked past the nurses' station and stopped at the fountain. She turned on the water and took a long drink. The familiar colorless spots were floating in front of her again and winging out into space. Anxiety attacks, Dr. Zimmerman had called these things.

She went across the hall to the waiting room and sat down on a couch. Sit it out and then leave fast, she told herself.

She looked around. Morbid atmosphere. Antiseptic reek. Every detail a reminder of last year, of Mike. And just when she had been beginning to get herself together, this accident had happened, which had seemed to touch her personally, even though she knew Gary less well than she knew a lot of her students. Senseless tragedy repeated with a new twist: Gary would live.

She leaned back on the couch and covered her face with her hands. Well, if there was something right to say to him in there, she hadn't said it. She had wanted to be warm and wise and had managed instead to come off ill at ease and boring. Even taking him a book struck her now as a mistake—a reminder of his physical limitations.

Ann stood up and tested herself. Not too shaky. On to the health club then. Swimming and marking a stack of compositions would give purpose to her evening. She put on her coat and went into the corridor. Neurosurgery floor: *We specialize in plugging unsightly holes in the head. Damaged spinal cords packed here for safe shipment elsewhere.* Gary, for instance, would be sent to Phillips Rehabilitation Institute as soon as his condition was stable. Go quickly, she told herself. Look straight ahead.

Ann pushed the button for the elevator. *When his condition was stable.* As if anything ever was stable. Gary had probably thought his move two weeks ago was pretty safe, stable. Routinely tackling a guy who ran back the second-half kickoff. That's what the teachers said who had been there. Nothing illegal on either side. No spear tackling. No defective headgear. Even the playback of the films hadn't shown anything unusual, according to Buck Lausch. A no-fault accident. The elevator arrived and carried her to the ground floor.

All quiet in the amber light of the entrance hall of St. Agnes Hospital. Just the statue of St. Agnes gazing down with polite condescension—and signs: VISITORS MUST CHECK IN. NO SMOKING. NO GARDEN FLOWERS PERMITTED FOR REASONS OF HEALTH. Walking past a row of potted plastic geraniums and through the revolving door, she inhaled fresh air. Enough of hospitals.

She went down the steps toward the parking lot.

"Hi."

Ann turned around. "Oh, hi," she said. It was Jason Lovett, hatless in the rain, leaning against the bus-stop sign. "Are you going downtown?" she asked.

"Yeah, to Allen Stereo."

Ann hesitated. "I'm going to Market and Appleton," she said. "Want a ride?"

"Sure. You'll pass right by."

She waited for Jason to catch up, and they walked in silence toward the car. Smooth kid. She had gathered that from seeing him around the halls at school. Good-looking. Poised.

"You going shopping?" he asked.

"No, swimming. I swim at least every other day."

"You in training or something?"

"I'm not Olympic material, if that's what you mean."

"So you do it to keep in shape—to keep your shape?"

"I do it for recreation. To work off pent-up energy. That's my car there," she said, "in case you forgot where I parked."

"I remember. Nice wheels," he said.

"They run." Ann unlocked the door, opened the other side, and waited for him to get in. "Actually I'm not much of a car person," she said, turning the key in the ignition. "Fasten your seatbelt, O.K.?"

Jason adjusted the belt, sat back. "I'm not a car person either. Not now. But someday, man. . . ."

Ann fumbled for quarters at the meter by the exit and pulled out onto the street. "Kids always see cars in their future," she said. "What else do you see?"

Jason looked at her appraisingly. "You really want to know, or is that just teacher jive?"

"Of course I want to know."

"Oh. O.K. Well, I see college on a football scholarship. Big Ten, probably, or Big Eight. I've been getting a lot of letters. Buck knows people. Got a long-distance call this morning from Oklahoma."

Ann looked at him. "Do you see an education as part of this Big Deal?"

"Hey. You are a *nasty teacher!* Do you take me for a bum?" He smiled.

"No," she said, "but you know the old story—athletes graduating, if they do at all, with A-plus in brawn and *F* in brains."

"Dumb jocks don't get that way in college, Ms. Treer. They're born that way."

She stopped for the light. "But you're made of finer stuff."

"You are a *mean lady*. I don't know what I'm made of yet, Ms. Treer. I'm only seventeen."

The traffic light turned green. "You're right," she said, "you've got plenty of time. Have you thought about what you're going to take in college?"

"Philosophy."

"Really?"

"I don't know. I just said that to mess up your stereotype."

"What stereotype?"

He laughed. "Any you might have."

Ann concentrated on the taillights of the car in front of her. "Do you mind my asking—how do you—how does the team feel about Gary, about the accident?" she asked.

"Oh, well—wow," Jason said. "There's no one way the

team feels. A couple of guys have thought of quitting. Nelson did quit. I guess he thought it could have been him next." Jason clasped and unclasped his hands. "Then you could say one jerk whose name I won't mention is happy about Gary, because now he'll get off the bench and play more. And Bill Berger, I hear, thinks maybe it was really his place to make that tackle, so he's feeling rotten. Some kids are fired up on account of Gary. They want to get revenge or win the season for him."

"And you?" They turned onto Market Street.

Jason shook his head. "None of that stuff. I always play to win, but I'll play the same as before—no harder or easier. I'd never quit because of being afraid to get hurt. I've already gotten wrecked a couple of times—my knee, broken collarbone."

"You figure you're safe—you've already had your share?"

"No, uh-uh. If I keep playing, I'll get roughed up more. I know that. That's the game. Football isn't some graceful dude throwing a pass downfield. It's knocking other guys down, sometimes hard enough so they don't get up, or *you* don't."

"Like Gary."

"Yeah."

She slowed for a light. "Do you like hitting, getting hit?" she asked.

"Yeah, I do," Jason said. " 'Football isn't a contact sport; it's a collision sport. Dancing is a contact sport.' That's what Vince Lombardi said. It's true. Colliding lets off steam—like you said about swimming."

She looked at him skeptically. "It's a whole other thing, isn't it?"

"I guess so. But believe it or not, I feel close to the guys I knock down. Women don't dig that."

"You're right. We don't." Ann rolled down her window and checked both ways before crossing the intersection. "Were you—are you close to Gary?" she asked.

Jason hunched his shoulders. "You'd have to ask him, I guess. I like Gary. Not that we've been that tight outside of school. But what I like is—Gary's different from the rest of the guys on the team. Doesn't always shoot his mouth off, like most of them animals. Hey, you know where Allen Stereo is?"

Ann nodded, pulled into the right-hand lane.

"I keep to myself in some ways, too," Jason said. "Maybe that's why I get along with Gary."

"Can you tell how he's taking this?"

"Uh-uh, not really. He puts up a good front. That's his way. But he doesn't know yet how it's going to turn out. Nobody does, far as I know. But if you ask me, it don't look good. Buck Lausch doesn't usually break down in the locker room."

"He did?"

"Yeah, day before yesterday. Everybody says not to spread it around, but I figure Buck can get away with it. Hell, even Joe Namath's cried in public. That's Allen's down there, Ms. Treer, O.K.?"

"Right. How did Buck happen to cry?"

"When he was praying for Gary."

"You pray in the locker room?"

"Buck does. A few guys mock him about it behind his back, but they all go along with him. He used to have a sign posted that said, 'Position on football field and in prayer—knees bent, eyes up,' but they made him take it down—the administration did. You know, separation of church and state, and all that crap. That's where I'm going, Ms. Treer. You can let me off on the corner."

Ann signaled and pulled over to the curb.

"I don't go in much for praying myself," Jason said, "but Buck's all right. I get along good with Buck." He opened the door.

"So long," Ann said.

"So long. I'll probably see you at the hospital or around school. Thanks for the ride."

"You're welcome. Good luck with your scholarships."

"Thanks." Jason got out, paused. "Swim hard," he called as he closed the door.

Ann pulled out into traffic. So long, Jason. Oh, boy. Football. Love that mayhem. And that *knees bent, eyes up*. Did it work for Buck Lausch? It hadn't worked for her, not for years. Come to think of it, she *could* picture Buck leading a prayer meeting in the locker room. Bash those Bears. Cream the Cougars. And then, Dear Father, please watch over Gary Madden.

Traffic ahead of her slowed. Ann turned on the radio to a bland, nothing station, the kind she'd been tuning in this last year in an attempt to avoid joyous or mean rock with its painful associations. What she got was a country-style song that made her remember in every detail Mike, standing in the living room, doing the folk-singer imitation he called Sheldon Clubfoot. She cut a laugh short and turned the dial to an all-news station. The windshield wipers beat like metronomes as she pulled into the lot on Appleton.

Health club relatively empty at five thirty. She entered the locker room and put on her bathing suit. O.K., go to it. Swim laps until you're numb, if possible. She plunged in, lifted her left elbow high out of the water, rolled her head, made a point of pulling her right arm down straight—like the arm of a paddlewheel. Her limbs were working together today, not like sometimes, when her right arm insisted on curving too much, or her legs wouldn't bear their share of effort. She switched to breaststroke, concentrated on keeping her kick symmetrical. Then she stopped pushing water, dragged her legs, let herself sink, rise slowly. Dead man's float. See what it's like? she teased her body. Paralysis. Muscles flaccid. The only thing was, when she got tired of drifting like a bloated fish, she could call those muscles to order again. And Gary couldn't. Action for Gary had been reduced to being turned like an ox on a spit, two hours up, two hours down.

Winding up with two laps of crawl, Ann got out of the pool. Drying herself vigorously, she watched an exercise class on the other side of the glass partition. A dozen women in three neat rows were bending and stretching in time to music. Women were sensible. They didn't bash their heads in and call it exercise. How come men did? Was it really biological, this need of men—of some men— to grapple on a sweaty mat, to hassle over a pigskin or race a hunk of steel? The surging of hormones—was it that simple?

She dressed quickly, anxious to get outside. It was a feeling she couldn't throw off, this wanting to get away from wherever she was, only to find the next person or place equally confining and boring. One of the main reasons she had married Mike—the only risky thing she'd ever done in her life—was because she knew she would never be bored with him. And she hadn't been, Ann thought, as she got into the car and drove down Appleton. Mike had charmed her in their two years together by always bringing home the unexpected, until the day he had gone out and met it and hadn't come back.

Lights in the lamp posts went on as she walked into her

building. In the mailbox, the letter from her parents would be urging her to please come home again this weekend.

She turned the key in the lock and switched on the lights in their apartment, so that the first familiar sight now, as every night, was the shelves Mike had sanded and stained; the rows of books that still carried invisible bookplates, his and hers; the print they had bought on their trip to Italy; the indestructible houseplant that Ellen and Jeff had given them. She could change everything, of course, or move to another apartment, but the thought left her weak and indecisive.

Ann dropped her things and turned on the radio to fill up the silence. Well, at least the visit to Gary was behind her. No need to go again. She could send cards to him from now on. Avoid pain—part of the hedonist code. Let Jason learn *that* in his study of philosophy.

She opened the refrigerator and stared, without appetite, at the contents. Mike would be annoyed if he could see her. He had taught her to cook well, to care about food. Now she had grown thin. She hated eating alone.

The telephone rang. Ellen, probably, with another invitation. Too much effort to go out. Say no. Ann picked up the receiver. "Hello."

"Ann, Buck Lausch here."

"Yes?" Odd.

"Listen, I'm sorry to bother you, especially when I know you were over there at the hospital and you probably just got in, but there's something I'd like to ask you that's come up."

"Yes?"

"Listen, Gary's in a bad way. You saw that for yourself, right? And here's the thing. We're trying to do all we can—money and so on. You know that. But one other item is his studies. I've just gotten off the phone with Mrs. Madden, and I agreed to organize this thing. She wants to get Gary started on his studies. I don't know if he can do them, but our feeling is we want him to think he can, and we want to send him his own teachers—you know what I mean, his regular teachers."

"You mean you want me to tutor him in English?"

"Yeah, that's the idea. Bedside instruction—two times a week beginning Monday. You for English and Crowell for math, Mrs. Purdy, and so on. It'll be supplemental pay, of course, but you'll have to go up to the hospital and then to the rehabilitation place if he's moved. So—"

"Wait a second—I—I don't know what to say. Starting Monday? Twice a—"

"Ann, the kid has to feel we're behind him. That's why the gate money from the game tomorrow is going to Gary. Some of my boys and I are taking it up there and presenting it to the family as soon as the game's over. And I'd like to be able to tell him his teachers are coming through, too. We want to make him think he can keep up."

"Can he?"

"Between you and me, I doubt it, but the mother thinks he can, so I'd like to see it done for her."

"Buck, this will probably sound selfish, and I don't mean it to be, but when I left the hospital this afternoon I made a decision not to go back for a while. For my own mental health, frankly."

"Ann, I know you've had one hell of a year, and I don't want to put pressure on you, but I wish to God you'd consider it. A team effort is what we need here." He paused. "You know the kid'll never walk."

"They know that? The doctor said so?"

"Kimball told me a couple of days ago. I'm sick, Ann.

One of my boys—a specimen like that—helpless as a baby."

"But they do therapy, right? I mean, some muscles come back—"

"Ann, look, Kimball's playing it straight when he says he can't say exactly until shock wears off, but he's ninety-nine percent sure there's permanent damage."

"Gary doesn't know, does he?"

"Nobody knows but his parents and me—one or two other people maybe. The kids don't know."

"When are they going to tell him?"

"The parents want to wait a little, another week or so, to make sure the condition is stable. So far he's taking it well, not asking too many questions. But they're going to have to tell him, and it's important that he be in the best possible spirits. So that's it, Ann. That's why we're trying like hell to do all we can."

"Yes." She allowed a buffer of silence. "I'd like to help, I really would," she said, knowing she was fighting to preserve a part of herself. "I'd like to help, but I don't think I can."

chapter **3**

"Isn't it wonderful that Mr. Lausch is going to try to get your own teachers to tutor you?"

"Yeah, it's great." Gary opened his mouth and swallowed the applesauce that his mother, kneeling on the floor, was spooning up at him through the opening in the frame. Weird, eating on the rack, flat on your stomach. "Is Dad coming soon?"

"Yes, any minute." Shifting her position, his mother lifted the spoon again. "It was nice of your friends to come up like that after the game this afternoon—with the game ball and the contribution. It's a good bit of money, you know."

"I know." Seemed like he hadn't stopped saying thank you for two solid weeks.

"And the big mirror works so well. I noticed you could see everybody this afternoon when they spoke to you."

"Yeah." Right now all he would be able to see was a white hump—the reflection of Tommy under a sheet.

"Who was the young man who presented the money, Gary?" his mother asked him.

"Jack Putnam."

"He seems like a nice boy."

"He fooled you, Ma," Gary said. Putnam the prick. The one guy on the team he couldn't stand. *You're going to come out of this thing a rich sonofabitch,* Putnam had joked as he left.

"I guess there're a lot of things that pass me by then," she said. "He looked like a nice young man to me. How about over there?" she asked, pointing to Tommy. "He's sleeping again, isn't he? I think they give him too many pain-killing pills," she whispered. "I'm glad they don't give you all those drugs."

"No need, Ma," he said. Feelin' no pain, that was him. He'd give anything for a twinge.

His mother raised the spoon to his mouth. "Diane's coming this evening, isn't that what you said? What time will she be here?"

"Soon. She's trying to get her parents' car, Billy told me before. She'll be up after supper." Hurry, Diane. Been looking forward all day.

"Oh, good." His mother got up. "Here comes Dad."

His parents were talking quietly at the door, the way they did every night. What were they saying? *Ask.*

"Hi, Gary, how's it going?"

27

"Hi, not bad." Through the opening he could see the bottoms of his father's trousers and polished shoes. His father was taking a step back from the frame now. It's O.K., Dad. You can come close. I won't bite.

"Your team won today, I hear."

"Yeah," Gary said. "6–0. They were happy. Billy scored the touchdown." Silence. Come on, must be something to talk about. "What did you do this afternoon?"

"Oh, I finished that accounting job. Watched the last half of the UCLA game."

"Who won?"

"UCLA, 14–10. I brought the newspaper. Want to hear the sports page?"

"Sure." His mother was still shoving food at him. He heard the rustle as his father folded back the newspaper. Exactly the same as every other suppertime at St. Agnes. The three of them. His mother feeding him tasteless food, trying to ask interesting questions. His father reading him the *New Bridge Herald* or *Sports Illustrated*. Hurry up, Diane.

" 'Losing is dull,' " his father was reading, " 'a fact which several teams in the NFL. . . .' "

What was going on in their heads? he wondered as he tuned out. *Two weeks now* and here he still was—his head alive and well and his body as good as dead. Were they getting panicked, too? Hard to tell, since they never showed their feelings much. Was his mother thinking, *I told you so?* She'd never exactly dug the idea of her only kid playing football, but she'd given in when she saw how big a kick Dad got out of it. Just about the only thing he and Dad had to talk about. What if he could never play football again—then what would they say to each other?

"This is the last spoonful, Gary. Oh, my, I've got to

stretch my legs for a minute. I'm not used to this bending."

Gary stared at the bare floor as his mother stood up. God, this whole thing must be tough on her. His father was at least leading a half-normal life, going to work as usual. But she was skipping her job down at the church, standing by him all day long. Ought to tell her he appreciated it. He'd never been good at saying those things though.

He heard a hum and his father stopped reading. Religion time at St. Agnes, once in the morning and once at night, out of the speaker on the wall.

"Hail Mary, full of grace, the Lord is with Thee . . ."

"These people make religion an integral part of their lives," his mother said.

These people, he thought. Jesus, Ma, Diane's one of *these people.* Their difference in religion probably bugged his mother a lot, though she'd never discussed it. Didn't bother him. Hell, he'd convert if Diane wanted him to.

"Blessed is the fruit of Thy womb, Jesus . . ."

"That reminds me," his mother whispered, "Pastor Shafer's coming to see you tomorrow morning, Gary."

"Yeah?" Like last Sunday, probably. Wanting to say the Creed with him. How could he say it without being a hypocrite? And how could he *not,* knowing they all cared so much?

"Pastor Shafer's been so good to us these last two weeks," his mother said.

"Yeah." Good to her, maybe, and his father. They dug Pastor Shafer. Shafer gave him the creeps. Hard to tell if he was alive or dead. A string of his sermons was like a losing season.

"He's interested in young people, Gary. He always wanted you in the youth group."

Her voice was shaky. Was she upset that he'd never joined the youth group? Maybe he would join, after this thing was over. If it'd make her happy.

"Now and at the hour of our death. Amen," said the voice on the P.A. The hum faded. The newspaper rustled again. His father was standing there ready to read.

"The nurse just brought a message from the switchboard, Gary," his father said, all of a sudden moving in close to the frame. "Diane says to tell you she's sorry but she can't make it over here tonight."

"Not at all?" Hell. Double hell. He felt the tears coming. *Don't show it.*

"That's a shame," his mother said.

Gary closed his eyes. Luckily they couldn't see his face. What the hell could it be with Diane—her parents? If she were sick and he were well, he'd overcome anything to see her. She'd sent the message with Billy that she was coming. So why hadn't she? He didn't pray often, but he had prayed she'd come. He had pictured looking at her in the mirror.

"That's too bad," his mother said, patting him on the shoulder. "But try not to mind, Gary, the three of us will have a nice evening together."

Well, they'd tried, anyway—tried *too hard*, if you asked him. He had wished his parents would just give up and admit the evening was a bust. But they'd stuck it out to the end of visiting hours. There was only one small lamp lit in the room now that they had gone. The corridor was still humming with night sounds—doctors being paged, nurses making rounds. The orderlies came in and flipped him. The bad time was coming closer. He heard a groan.

"Hey, man, what's your name again?"

"Gary. How're you doing?"

"Lousy now, but I'll be flying soon. They just gave me some St. Agnes Special Sauce."

"You got pain?"

"Hell, yeah."

"Where?"

"My back, around T-10."

"T-10?"

"That's what they call it. The bone where I hit."

"How'd you do it?"

"Flew off a cycle."

"When?"

"A couple of months ago."

"How'd it happen?"

"My buddy and I took a challenge to race these two cats up Route 21. We were doing eighty—him driving and me on the back—and we—we must've hit a rock or something on the road. My buddy, he sailed one way, I went the other. I went over a what-do-you-call-it—a bridge abutment —and landed on my back. They didn't find me for eight hours."

"What about the other guy?"

"They found him first. Took him to Cortland General. That's were I had my operation."

"Guess you'll never ride a motorcycle again."

"The hell I won't. Another buddy of mine's selling me his as soon as I get out."

"That's crazy," Gary said.

"No, it ain't. What'd *you* do to rack yourself up?"

"Football."

"That's not crazy? Look, here's the thing—would you play again?"

Gary hesitated. "I'd . . . sure as hell give it a lot of

thought first," he said, "but . . . yeah, I probably would."

"Well then, who's crazy? Whew, I'm gonna go under in a minute. If I fade out on you, no offense, O.K.? They cut me, you know."

"Cut you?"

"Yeah, a spinal fusion. They weld your back together. They join two thingamajigs. They graft something. How do I know what they do? All I know is it hurts like hell."

"You'll be O.K.?"

"O.K.? You mean walk?"

"Yeah."

"I'd better. Because if I can't walk somehow, man, you're not gonna see me around here long, and when I say 'around,' I don't just mean around bloody St. Agnes. Hey, I've had it. Wooo . . . sweet dreams . . . what's your name?"

"Gary."

Tommy slept. Gary breathed quickly. Panic time. Fewer and fewer noises in the hall, all of them magnified. Every whisper was one nurse telling another something awful about a patient—something the poor slob didn't know. Every rush of footsteps was toward some guy taking his last breath. Sleep tight, Tommy Frechette. Lucky S.O.B., with your Special Sauce. Hey Tommy, gimme some?

Gary closed his eyes. Darkness. No movement. No feeling from the shoulders down. Wasn't this about as close as you could come to being dead? He played a game: Your body's dead, Madden, but your superior brain lives on. Ruthless Dr. Kimball is waiting for this moment. He covets your brain for his experiments. At midnight he'll come with the cart . . . and the knife. . . . Gary opened his eyes. He could feel sweat on his forehead. Hot in here. Maybe he had a temperature. Easy to catch something with your resistance wiped out. Easy to die. . . . *Local Athlete Succumbs to Injuries.* Gary Madden, New Bridge football hero, died last night at St. Agnes Hospital after—No, not that . . . picture something good: It's spring and he's almost well. Still walking with crutches, but he's used to them. At school kids open doors for him. His shoulders are massive from using the crutches. It's early evening. He and Diane are in River Park at that secluded spot. He lets his crutches fall to the ground. He can walk!

"Come here," Diane says, leading him into a lean-to of evergreens. Her eyes are shining. She smiles and steps out of her dress. "I've been waiting for this moment for a long time," she says. "I only waited because I wanted it to be right."

Now Diane was calling to him from the top of a steep cliff. He was climbing, but he kept tripping over rocks and roots of trees. He fell, rolled over. . . .

"You're O.K., Gary," the orderly said gently. "We're turning you. You can go back to sleep in a minute."

He was on his stomach, dozing again. Now he was running the length of the field, flinging himself into the air, hitting Lionetti . . . going down. . . .

"No!" he shouted. Suddenly he was up, on his feet in his own living room. "I was dreaming, wasn't I?" he asked his mother. "It didn't really happen—the accident—did it?"

"Yes," she said, her voice trembling.

"Why?"

"God's testing us. He's testing us because he loves us so much."

He woke with a start. Where was his mother? Now he understood how a person could go crazy. Stretch a guy out flat, keep him in suspense about what was wrong with him, wake him every time he fell asleep, and leave him alone with his own head. That could do it, easy.

Was it real, what he saw now? People who were going crazy had hallucinations. But this wasn't a hallucination—this was real. A form in his mirror.

"Who is it?" he asked. No one answered. The form didn't move. Was it Tommy Frechette? "Tommy?" he called. Nothing. Better go take a look over there across the room.

The tongs came out of his head painlessly. He dropped the weights to the floor. His arms moved with ease and he got off the frame. God, what a relief. He had thought he was paralyzed! He walked away from the mirror toward the form that lay under a sheet on a slab of marble. Should he touch it? He had to know who—

"Tommy?" he called again. He took a step closer, lifted the corner of the sheet, ripped it away. Oh, my God! The body lay facedown, the back split from the base of the neck to the tailbone, like a butchered animal.

"They cut him!" Gary heard himself saying. "He *told* me they cut him." He looked with revulsion at the bloody body. Was it Tommy? He had to be sure. He put out his hand to touch the damp hair, then he rolled the head over. "No—no—" he said softly, and as he said it the body faded away. But he had seen enough to know for sure that the face he had looked into was his own.

Gary, waking in a sweat, gasped for breath. Hoping by sheer concentration to will himself to another time and place, he closed his eyes once more and wished himself in New Bridge High School. Nothing to worry about—when he opened his eyes again, he'd be sitting in class. Then, calling on all the strength he'd stored up from a thousand afternoons of working out, he strained his muscles. His neck moved slightly. But when he opened his eyes, all he saw was the small patch of vinyl floor in the early morning light. He was exactly where he had been for two weeks— on the frame in St. Agnes Hospital.

chapter 4

Ann Treer stood in the doorway of her classroom. Monday was over. The seniors were frantic to escape.

"Hand me your essays," she said as the bell rang. "Please don't throw them on my desk." She grabbed and shuffled papers, stepped inside as the students rushed out.

" 'Bye, Ms. Treer, have a good day!"

"Thanks." She'd try, anyway. That was one resolve of the weekend, to try to have good days. Another resolve had been to call Buck Lausch and tell him that she'd changed her mind. Women's prerogative, right, Buck? She'd tutor Gary. Not fair to make the kid adjust to a new teacher at a time like this. So what if she hated hospitals, wanted to avoid pain, had personal problems. Didn't everybody?

She'd skip swimming this afternoon and give Gary a short session on *Crime and Punishment*.

Lockers slammed in the hall, feet stomped, the crescendo of voices peaked and diminished. Ann went to her desk.

"I'm almost finished, Ms. Treer." Dennis Fagin was still writing after everybody else had left. "O.K.? Want to see it?"

"I'll wait until you're done," she said. One of those kids who called her over to check every sentence as he wrote it.

"I'm done now!"

"Good." Ann got up and looked at his paper. "You've stuck pretty much to what we said in class," she said.

"Yeah? Terrific." Dennis beamed.

Her own fault that he took it as a compliment. She'd been letting him get away with being dependent.

"So long, Ms. Treer," he said, pulling on his jacket. "See you tomorrow. No homework, right?"

"Right. We're starting something new."

"So there's nothing for tomorrow?"

"No, Dennis."

"O.K., then. Have a good day, Ms. Treer."

"You too."

Ann gathered her books. On to the hospital. She got her coat from the closet.

"Ms. Treer?"

A girl in a hooded car coat stood at the door.

"Are you Ms. Treer?"

"Yes." The girl looked familiar. Tall, blond.

"Ms. Treer, can I see you for a second?"

"Sure. You're—"

"We just met for a second. I'm Diane. Diane Lacey, Gary's girl friend."

"Oh, yes. I saw you at the hospital on Friday. Come on

in. Put your books down." Ann laid her coat on the desk. "What can I do for you?" she asked.

"Mr. Lausch told me you were going to tutor Gary today," Diane said distractedly. "Are you?"

"Yes."

"Could you take him a letter?" She began rifling through the pages of a notebook.

"I'd be glad to. You're not going up?"

"No, I've got to go to work. Gary knows it. I wrote him this letter in class." She set the notebook on the desk and turned pages. "Where is it now?" Holding the book upside down, she shook it. "This is all I need. . . ."

"Can I help?"

"No," she said with one last shake. "I can tell it's not here. Where could I have dropped it? I wrote it in home ec—" She sat down and examined the notebook once more. "This is the last straw—honestly. . . ."

Ann went through Diane's stack of books. "If it's really lost," she said, "maybe you could write another one. I'll wait."

Diane pushed the notebook aside as if she hadn't heard. "Oh, Ms. Treer, I don't know what's wrong with me. You don't even know me, so you must think I'm crazy." She put her head down.

Ann watched her in silence. Poor kid. Face of a child, body of a woman. She was crying. "What can I do to help?" Ann asked quietly.

Diane looked at her, her eyes wet. "I didn't mean to come in here and act like this, Ms. Treer, but I can't help it. I'm so mixed up. I'm so tired. I keep losing things. I keep being late for work so they'll probably fire me. Even Gary's mad at me."

"Why?"

"That's the thing, I'm not even sure. Saturday night I couldn't get up to see him. My parents needed the car, and I would've had to walk, and they didn't want me out by myself—"

"Didn't Gary understand that?"

"No, but that's not the only thing. At first he was so glad to see me, when he was in Intensive Care. And even when other people started coming to visit, he wanted to see me most, I could tell. But yesterday he was like a stranger." She paused. "Do you think I'm crazy, Ms. Treer, for telling you all this?"

"No, why would I?"

Diane played with the ring on a chain around her neck. "*I'm* not acting any different than before. I won't go out with anybody else. I told him that. I'll wait for him. I want him to tell me everything about how he feels, but I don't think he wants to talk about it."

"He's going through something we can hardly imagine," Ann said.

"I know. That's why I wish he'd open up," Diane said. "He's always been quiet, but with those tongs, and other people always there, we can't discuss anything, not even on the phone. I have nobody to talk to. I guess that's why I'm going on like this to you."

"That's all right," Ann said. "I don't know if I can say anything that'll help you, but you don't have to worry about what I think. Isn't it good for Gary just for you to be there, even if you don't talk much?"

"I *wish*," Diane said. "But that's not the way it is."

"What do you mean?"

"His mother won't let me near him. She does everything. I wanted to feed him yesterday, but she said she'd do it. She doesn't trust me."

"I doubt that," Ann said. "It's just that people get into patterns. She's been doing everything from the start—"

"She doesn't like me, Ms. Treer."

"What makes you think that?"

"'I see it now that she never liked me. Before, I always thought I imagined it. It didn't matter before—usually Gary came over to my house. But now, with this, I see it's true, Ms. Treer, she doesn't like me!"

Ann hesitated. "Try to look at it from her point of view. A thing like this happening so suddenly to her only child. Think how hard it must be on her."

"If it's hard on her," Diane said, "then she should accept help."

Ann glanced at the clock. "Diane," she said, "write Gary another letter. Go on."

Diane tore a page from her notebook and began. Ann watched her. Big, round script. Circles over the *i*'s. Generous, uncomplicated, a dreamer, the handwriting analysts would probably say. She was the kind of kid who probably wrote S.W.A.K. on the back of envelopes. The kind who'd have a chenille bedspread with a stuffed something on it, which Gary with mixed pleasure and embarrassment would have been conned into giving her for her birthday. A picture of him in his football uniform pinned on her bulletin board. What would she do with that memento now?

Diane crossed out a sentence, crumpled up the sheet of paper, and took another one from the notebook.

"Be quick," Ann said, "the Pony Express is leaving."

Diane wrote. The message was obvious, even upside down: "I love you, Your Diane." She folded it in quarters and gave it to Ann.

"He's such a good person, Ms. Treer!" Diane said, a

floodgate of feeling opening. She put her head down on the desk and cried softly.

Ann came closer and rested her hand on Diane's arm. "It's O.K.," she said.

"What'll I do?"

"Do you feel comfortable enough to talk to Mrs. Madden? Can you tell her you want to help?"

"In front of Gary?"

"No, in the waiting room, maybe, or ask if you can come by the house to talk to her."

Diane shook her head, sniffed. "I don't see myself doing it, Ms. Treer. She scares me."

"It can't be that bad," Ann said. "I know it might be hard to bring up the subject, but why don't you try to talk to her?"

Diane wiped her face. "I'll be late for work."

"You don't have to speak to her now," Ann said. "Do it tomorrow. Anytime. It's worth trying, right? For Gary's sake?"

"Maybe," she said. "Thanks, Ms. Treer." She gathered her books and stood up. "You've been—thanks for listening. Who knows what you must be thinking. I didn't mean to come in here and—"

"Don't worry about it, Diane. Come anytime. Can I give you a ride to work on my way to the hospital?"

"No, thanks. I've got a ride today." Diane stood in the doorway. "Give the note to him right away, Ms. Treer, O.K.? Before you tutor? Tell him I'll be there tomorrow no matter what."

"I will."

Diane left. Where would it end with her and Gary? Ann wondered. Or maybe it wouldn't end. Sometimes crisis brought out the best in people. Ann picked up her briefcase and walked through the empty halls to the parking lot.

As she walked to her car, she glanced toward the field where the team was running drills. There was Jason, and there was Buck yelling at some kids attacking dummies. "Harder! Lower!" Had anything changed? she wondered. Did Buck hold his breath now with every hit? Or did he still buy the old Lombardi slogan that Mike had often quoted: "Hurt is in your mind"?

Ann got into her car and turned the key in the ignition. What kept Buck going on with it? The fact that most kids *didn't* get injured? Probably with him it was a blend of faith in God and statistics. Mike had had little use for the former but great enthusiasm for the latter. Over a million players in organized tackle football every season, he'd always told her, and only a handful of serious injuries or deaths. You had a better chance of killing yourself in a bathtub or—or of getting killed in a car. He had even trusted the odds on that, but they had played him false, so that Mike, an admirer of statistics, had become one.

Ann drove down MacIver Street. Keep the tutoring short, she reminded herself. Raise a few questions about *Crime and Punishment* for him to think about until the next time: Why are the worst punishments the ones we inflict on ourselves? What changes in behavior can we attribute to the power of love? She'd stick to the regular syllabus as much as possible but alter it to suit his needs and restrictions. His new life would have to be contemplative. What should she ask him to contemplate?

Ann drove along the river to the hospital. The weather was clear. The place looked more ordinary, more human, this time around. She went inside and in the elevator an orderly moved over to make room for her. Getting off at the third floor, she walked down the corridor, only faintly aware of antiseptic. Mrs. Madden was standing outside Gary's room.

"Hello," Ann said. "How's Gary?"

Mrs. Madden intercepted her. "Mrs. Treer . . ." Her mouth twitched. "I'm afraid we've caused you some inconvenience."

"No, not at all."

Mrs. Madden leaned forward nervously. "This problem came up too late to get in touch with you at school. I'm afraid we can't start tutoring today."

"Oh, I'm sorry. Is it something serious?"

She turned her face away. "Would you mind terribly coming back Wednesday? I'm so sorry to cause you this bother, but I'm sure that everything will be fine by then."

"Of course. I'll come back Wednesday. But—is it—is there anything at all I can do now?"

"No, Mrs. Treer," she said, looking at her. "You know, until now Gary's been in such good spirits. We've done everything possible to assure that. But—and I'm convinced this is temporary—he's not—feeling like himself today for some reason. He hasn't eaten. And—I'm sure there's nothing personal, Mrs. Treer—he refuses to have his tutoring session. The doctor's not here right now, but the nurse agrees with me—we can't force him."

"I guess not," Ann said. "I'm sorry to hear that." She hesitated. "Well, let me know if—if it's not all right for Wednesday. I hope he feels better."

"I'm counting on it," Mrs. Madden said. "He's a strong boy. Good-bye, Mrs. Treer."

Ann walked quickly down the hall. Strong mother, strong son. But the strain was showing on both of them. How come he'd refused to be tutored? Nothing personal, his mother had said, but naturally she would want to avoid embarrassment. Maybe Gary had hoped for a different teacher. But more likely, Gary was figuring out a few things for himself, was looking farther into the future than his mother wanted him to and was asking himself what he was being tutored for.

Ann pushed the elevator button impatiently. She hurried out the door and across the lot and didn't remember until later, when she was in the middle of swimming laps, that she had forgotten to deliver the note from Diane.

chapter **5**

Gary stared at the screen of his new TV reflected in the mirror. Daytime shows—garbage. He closed his eyes. Well, he'd gotten away with it. No tutoring. It was easier than he figured, getting out of doing things. He'd been tempted at the last minute to call his mother and tell her to bring Treer in. But what the hell. He didn't feel like it. He had read a little of *Crime and Punishment* with his prism glasses, but he was tired, and he still had a long way to go. He wouldn't mind discussing hallucinations like the one Raskolnikov had just had, but how was he supposed to keep all those other Russian names straight? Not a bad book, but he couldn't face it now. Didn't feel like facing anything.

That's how he'd gotten into this—game, or whatever it was. First he hadn't felt like drinking his water this morning. And when he hadn't felt hungry at breakfast, his mother had made such a big deal about it that it had annoyed him. Why did she come to the hospital so early anyway? If he was really getting better, why was it necessary? So he'd refused lunch, too. Maybe if Tommy had been in the room they would have talked a little, and he would have gotten out of this mood, but Tommy was down in physical therapy.

Anyway, around two o'clock Dottie, the sexy physical therapist, had come around, and he'd said he didn't want therapy. She'd be back, though. She was a tough nut to get rid of. He'd have to stand firm. Ha. Stand firm. It was amazing how many expressions sounded like sick jokes when you were in the hospital: Sit up and take notice. Stand up for your rights. You don't have a leg to stand on. Oh yeah, he had two. They just weren't working, was the problem.

The fact that he wasn't eating was really bugging his mother. She was uptight because he'd already lost weight. "Should I call Dr. Kimball?" he'd heard her ask Sister Marie, but Kimball was out of town for a couple of days, and some other guy was on call. Good—let them phone Kimball long-distance. He'd love to see Kimball right now and ask him straight out: How long? When will I walk? He'd meant to yesterday, but Kimball hadn't given him a chance. This was getting ridiculous. The frame was too narrow for him. There was a little bleeding where the tongs were set in his head. But that stuff was nothing compared to the being-done-to. The orderly sticking a red rubber Foley tube in your cock. The nurse poking up your ass. And worst of all: *still no new movement.* Come on, Kimball, you bastard, what's the story?

So one thing had led to another and he had refused to see Treer. His mother had tried to talk him into it, but he'd won. Now he wasn't so sure, though. He opened his eyes. Almost anything, even a crummy discussion of Russian names, would be better than lying here watching a soap opera. Right this minute two fakey-looking women were sitting there on their butts in Soaptown drinking coffee and worrying about whether their husbands were off having affairs. He hoped they were. Women deserved it. They were pains in the ass.

Especially Diane. What the hell was wrong with her? At first she'd been great. Even the interns had kidded him about Diane hanging around the ICU, and during the first couple of days after that, she'd been here whenever she wasn't in school. But then she'd stood him up last Saturday night and had only stayed a short time yesterday. Not that he'd expected her to stick around day and night like his mother did. But she could have found some way to get here Saturday. *She* had two legs to walk with, didn't she?

Wait a minute. Diane wasn't lazy. Saturday night wasn't really what was bugging him. It was more the way she'd acted yesterday—bashful, sort of, as if she'd rather let his mother take over. Was she turned off by seeing him like this? Or was she just getting impatient? Diane had said she wouldn't think of going out with anybody else while he was sick. Maybe she was seeing already what a drag that was.

Anyway, forget women. Practically all he saw all day long were women. His mother forcing food on him. The flying nun flipping him. Other nurses measuring his pee. Dottie cracking his bones. Treer—yeah. Another one, if he had let her in. Glad he hadn't. Meanwhile, where were

47

some *men*, for God's sake? He couldn't take this life in the Ladies' Aide Society much longer. Kimball? Away at a conference. His father was at work. Billy, visiting a college. Thank God for Buck and Jason, anyway, but they could only come to see him after practice. The TV ladies were still yakking. He didn't care if he never saw another woman. Except one.

He heard footsteps. "Mom?"

"Yes?"

"Could you switch the channel?" If he really wanted to follow through with this negative bit, he shouldn't ask for a thing.

His mother turned the dial. "What would you like to see?"

Her voice was soft, the way he remembered it from when he was a little kid in bed with flu. Shouldn't be so obnoxious to her. "A movie, maybe," he said, "or a talk show."

A Kentucky Fried Chicken commercial came on, and she kept the channel. "That looks good," she said. "Do you think you'll eat a little something this evening, Gary?"

Damn. Couldn't she be less obvious? Couldn't she just let him alone?

"I called Dad," she said, "and asked him to bring a milkshake when he comes."

A bribe. "I'm not hungry," he said.

She came over to the bed and put her hand on his forehead. "Does your head hurt?" She smoothed his hair.

His hair hadn't been washed all this time. At home she always mocked him about washing it every night like a girl in a shampoo ad. Now it was itchy, and even though it was shorter than usual, he could see when they held a mirror close that strands of it were glued together. That must be it. Diane was turned off by the way he looked. She had told him he looked good, but how could she mean it—skin dead-white, losing weight, oily hair? In war movies girls dug wounded guys looking pale and heroic, but this was no war movie.

"Gary . . ."

There was that hesitation again in her voice.

"Is there anything you want to talk about?" she asked.

"No." Why had he said it so fast? Here she was, trying, and he wasn't giving her a chance. It was the way she did it, though. It reminded him of how both of them—his father, too—had told him about sex. They had come up to him once or twice, like two members of a committee that neither of them really wanted to serve on, and said: "Is there anything you want to ask us about sex?" He had always said no. Hell, it was easier to get it from books.

"Is there anybody you'd like to see, Gary—anybody you'd like to talk to?"

"No." Could have said Diane. Could say Dr. Kimball. But Diane was at work, and if he asked outright for Kimball, it would look like he was scared. And he didn't want them to think that.

"How about Diane?" his mother said.

"What about her?" Keep talking.

"Would you like me to get in touch with her and see if she can come over?"

He cleared his throat. "She's at work," he said slowly.

"Oh."

Gary watched his mother's face. Yeah, he felt like saying, call Diane at work and tell her it's urgent. He pictured her getting the call.

"Well," his mother said, as if her mind were someplace else, "if she's working, I guess we shouldn't disturb her."

Come on, Ma, he wanted to shout. Let's disturb Diane! But he wouldn't. Wouldn't beg for Diane.

"I'll be back in a minute," his mother said.

What was she up to? Going to call Diane? Go ahead, Ma. Maybe she could read his mind better than he thought. He glanced at the reflection of TV again. His mother had forgotten to find him a movie, and a rerun of a game show was on now—"To Tell the Truth." Three suave guys with mustaches were all claiming to be stunt pilots, but two of them were lying. Just like TV, to make a game out of who was the best liar. Some people around this place ought to go on that show. Tommy Frechette, for instance. He could tell some good ones. Or Kimball . . .

He heard voices in the hall. His mother again, talking to someone. Couldn't be Diane. Impossible. Somebody was coming in, though. Hell! Dottie the therapist. Stand firm.

"Hi, Gary! How are you, bubby?"

She came close enough so he could smell her cologne.

"Feeling better?" She lifted his left arm.

How could he get rid of her?

"Let's keep things moving." She smiled.

She wasn't giving him a chance. Her tight red curls brushed against his face as she rotated his elbow.

Cut it out! he felt like saying. Hell, useless as it was, it was *his* body. She'd moved right in and taken over. How did she paint on those weird eyes, anyway? he wondered.

She did the range of motion on his wrist, then his elbow. "Hon," she said, "you're getting more elbow flexion, you know that? Can you tell?"

"Yeah?"

"Try to move your wrist. Come on now. You're going to get that back soon. I have a feeling." Dottie looked at him. "Hey, I saw your girl friend here the other day. What a great-looking chick. What's her name?"

"Diane."

"Have you gone with her long?"

"Since last school year."

Dottie was working on his fingers now. It was too late to stop her.

"Are you two both seniors? In the same classes?" Dottie asked.

"Yeah, we're seniors. We're not in any classes together this year. I met her in a class, though, last spring—health ed."

"You mean sex education?"

Gary smiled. "Well, that was part of the course."

"You met during that part, huh? What's Diane going to do after she graduates?"

"Go to college, I guess. She wants to be a social worker or a dental hygienist, something like that. She's good with people." Funny he was saying that after spending the day cursing out Diane. It was true, though. She was great with people. That's what had attracted him.

Dottie switched to his right arm. "You've sure had a lot of visitors, Gary. I'm impressed. All those fellas from your team. Who's your best friend—I mean *boy* friend?"

"Well, Bill Berger's my oldest buddy, since something like second grade. He's a good guy. I got a lot of friends—"

"Hey, bubby, your mom's coming. Let's show her your elbow flexion. Mrs. Madden—"

How about that. He *was* moving his elbow a little when Dottie helped. His mother appeared in the mirror.

"Gary, I have something for you," she said. She was holding a folded piece of paper. "Mrs. Treer was nice enough to come back with this, Gary. It's a note from Diane that Mrs. Treer was supposed to deliver. She came all the way back. Wasn't that considerate?"

"From Diane?"

"Yes, do you want your prism glasses?"

Dottie winked. "Give it to me, Mrs. Madden." She grabbed the note from her. "O.K., Gary, if you want this, you'll have to reach for it."

"Come on." He smiled.

Dottie held the note a few inches above his right hand where it lay on his abdomen. "*You* come on," she said. "Flex that elbow. Lift. Otherwise I'll read it myself and I won't tell you what it says."

Gary moved his shoulder. "Come on," he said, "you've got to be kidding."

"I'm serious!" Dottie laughed.

"Let him have it," Mrs. Madden said. "I'll hold it for him."

"Nothing doing. Move your elbow two measly inches and *I'll* hold the letter for you."

Gary concentrated. Pretend it's morning. Fresh start. Just woke up. O.K., nothing to it. Lift the old elbow! His shoulder muscles ached. He strained as hard as he could. Looking in the mirror, he watched with fascination as he raised his elbow the slightest bit for a half a second. Not two inches, but something.

"Terrific! See!" Dottie kissed him on the forehead.

"Good!" his mother said. "That's wonderful! Wait til Dad sees that!"

Gary's arm lay flaccid again on the sheet, but Dottie was holding the notebook paper above him, and he had read the message.

"Thanks," Gary said.

"Short and sweet, huh?" Dottie said.

Gary smiled. "She gets right to the point."

"Gary," his mother said, "Mrs. Treer's still out in the hall. That woman's so patient. She wants to know if you have an answer for Diane."

"Tell her . . . that Gary says 'Same here. Come soon.' "

" 'Same here come soon?' " she repeated. "Any message for Mrs. Treer?"

"Yeah, thanks a lot—and—I'll see her Wednesday."

chapter 6

Ann put her foot on the accelerator. Tutoring after school was always tough. Now that she had agreed to it, she'd try to be gracious, but teaching one-to-one was exhausting, even when you were fresh and the student was willing and able. Who knew what shape she'd find Gary in?

Ann turned onto River Drive. Gary was eating normally again, Buck had told her, and he'd gotten some movement in his right arm from working with the therapist. How much should she ask of Gary? A minimum, if she went along with the other teachers. Crowell and Purdy were planning to treat the tutoring as a rubber-stamp job. If Gary's mind was in order, though, wouldn't she be insulting him by not making him use it?

A siren wailed as she drove onto the hospital grounds. The whirling red light of an ambulance flashed in her face. She parked the car and walked toward the entrance.

Stepping out on the third floor, she noticed that Mrs. Madden wasn't guarding the door. A good sign. Ann knocked.

"Come in," Mrs. Madden called.

She entered the room. Mrs. Madden, placing a marker in a book, stood up. "Hello, there," she said. "I've just been reading a little to Gary. The glasses make him tired."

"Hello," Ann said. "Hi, Gary."

"Hi."

He lay face up on his frame as before, but he was noticeably thinner and whiter. "Good to see you," she said. She took off her coat and hung it on a hook. She moved close to the frame and glanced at the other bed. "How's your roommate?" she asked.

"Sleeping," Gary said. "He's taking a lot of medication. He sleeps a lot."

"Let me get a chair," Mrs. Madden said.

Ann looked at the stool by the Stryker frame. "Oh, that'll be fine."

"Well, I thought I'd stay for at least part of the lesson," Mrs. Madden said. "In case you need me for anything, or Gary—"

Ann hesitated. "Oh, that won't be necessary! We'll be all right."

"Sometimes Gary needs water. He has to drink—"

"Mrs. Madden," Ann interrupted, "you must be tired. This is a good chance for you to go down to the coffee shop and take a break." She surprised herself by the cheerful firmness of her tone. "I can give Gary water if he needs it. You go on now."

"I like to stay close by," Mrs. Madden said half apologetically.

"You've been putting in such long days," Ann said. She felt as if she were staring her down. "Go. Please." Ann held her smile until Mrs. Madden looked away.

"Well, all right," Mrs. Madden said. "That's very kind of you."

Ann sat on the stool. "Take your time," she called. "I'll come down and tell you when I'm leaving."

Mrs. Madden paused. "I'll be back, Gary," she said. She picked up her purse and went out.

"Man, you're the first person who's convinced her to go all the way downstairs," Gary said.

His voice was thin, hollow. His skin seemed translucent. Here by herself, so close, Ann was struck by an otherworldly quality about him. "I hear you're moving your arm," she said.

"Yeah, I'm flapping one wing a little. See?" He twitched his elbow.

"Great. Just the one side?"

"Yeah." His eyes roamed the ceiling. "Bring me another letter from Diane and I'll move the left one. I moved my right arm Monday, you know, when the therapist made me try to reach for that note you delivered. Thanks, by the way."

"You're welcome," Ann said. "If I'd known the power of it, I would've locked Diane in a room until she filled it up with letters."

"You mean like that fairy tale"—his voice trailed off—"where the girl spins straw into gold. . . ."

"Right," Ann said. "*Rumpelstiltskin*. Well, anyway, I'm locking Diane in a room tonight."

"Make it this one."

"What?" Ann smiled.

"Nothing."

"I heard you." She looked at his eyes, sunken and brilliant. "It must get lonely," she said, dropping her guard.

Gary sighed. "It's—not too bad."

"Do they have you doing much physical therapy?" she asked.

"*They* do most of it. They move my joints. They give me chest physical therapy—got to learn to cough all over again. And they examine every inch of my skin for redness so I don't get decubiti—bedsores. I'm learning all these fancy words."

"Then you don't need me for vocabulary, right?"

"Right. We can just skip tutoring."

"No, I mean we can spend all our time on literature."

"I figured you'd get around to that. Come on, Ms. Treer, do I have to read that book?"

"*Crime and Punishment?* Sure!" That had always been her response to "Do we have to . . ." questions. In this case, though, should he have to?

"Why?" he asked.

She tapped her fingers on the edge of the frame. In this setting the answer seemed more crucial and elusive than ever. "Why? Because you're a senior in a college-prep English class. Because literature widens your view of the world. Because *Crime and Punishment* has held up for a lot of years. Because Raskolnikov is, to some extent, all of us." Ann stopped. The same tired rhetoric. She recognized it. He would, too.

Gary's voice came from far away. "I never murdered anybody like he did."

"Right," she said. "Raskolnikov's all of us in the sense that he feels deprived, as we all do sometimes. He deludes

himself into thinking he's special. As a result, he decides it's
O.K. for him to commit a crime. But he can't live with it.
He's haunted by guilt, as many people are. He . . ." She
watched Gary's eyes wandering. No wonder. Her voice was
boring even her. Should she, after all, force a kid who had
barely escaped death, a kid who couldn't move his head
or hold a book, a kid who would never walk and didn't
know it yet, to finish a 510-page, often-depressing novel
about a murderer? Maybe Crowell and Purdy were right.
Give the kid a break.

"Did you go to the game Saturday, Ms. Treer?"

"No, I didn't," she said. "But I heard we won." He was
sensing her uncertainty, taking advantage by changing the
subject, the oldest trick in a student's repertoire.

"Undefeated." He watched her hopefully. "What do you
think of that?"

"I think . . ." He'd spent half his life talking about football—that was going to have to change. "I think the team
must be working hard," she said, "just like you're going to,
in English."

"Ms. Treer," he groaned, "I mean, *that book!* All those
names! I can't keep them straight!"

"I'll explain the variations. They're completely logical.
We'll make a chart."

"Yeah, I'll keep a chart," he said sarcastically.

"Diane will help you," she said. "I'll get Diane. Your
mother shouldn't have to deal with details like this."

"When will you get her to come?"

"As soon as possible. Before the next lesson. Tomorrow,
I hope."

"And how long will I have to finish the book?"

"Don't worry about the deadline now. We'll take as
much time as you need."

Gary sighed again. "So I have to do it . . ."

Ann studied his face, took a chance that she was guessing right. "Yes," she said.

"Then what? What do I read then, after *Crime and Punishment?* If I'm still not back in school . . ."

"Well," Ann said, "some plays by Ibsen, composition—"

"The class already started *Death of a Salesman,* didn't they? I'm doing that too, aren't I?"

"Probably." He was a step ahead of her. She hadn't wanted to lay on too much depressing reading, but he was testing to see if he was a special case.

"Better give me that *Death of a Salesman,* too," he said. "I may as well keep up with everything. That way I'll be better off when I come back."

"Right," she said. "That's why I want you to keep a journal like the rest of the class is doing."

"A journal?"

"A notebook that you'll eventually write in. For the time being, I'll ask Diane to take dictation from you, and maybe you can use the tape recorder sometimes."

"What do I dictate?"

"Your ideas. Most of the time the subject will be up to you. The main purpose is to improve writing. Even if you aren't doing the writing yourself at first, it'll be practice in organizing your thoughts."

"What thoughts?"

"Whatever interests you. What you do here. A comment on something you see on television. A profile of someone here at the hospital. Anything. If it happens to be personal and you don't want me to read it, just have Diane write 'personal' on the page, and I'll respect that. I don't have to inspect every word. The point of it is to exercise your mind."

"How long does it have to be?"

"One side of notebook paper per day."

"That much?"

"Oh, come on. That's nothing. Besides, I've seen Diane's handwriting. It's huge."

Gary smiled. "How do you know her writing?"

"I saw it when she wrote your name on the note," Ann said, "and if I don't know her writing now, I will by the time we're finished with this, won't I?"

"Yeah. Hey, Ms. Treer. Could you get me my water, please? Just fill the cup from the pitcher."

"Sure." She poured the water and inserted a straw. As she bent over Gary's bed, a strange wave came over her. At first she mistook it for the familiar anxiety attack. But it wasn't that. It wasn't a negative sensation at all. Quite the opposite, in fact. She felt airy, vital, and vulnerable. "Is that enough water?" she asked gently.

"Yes. Thanks."

Ann sat down and the wave passed, leaving her light-headed. "Let's talk a little about *Crime and Punishment*," she said.

"How about some other book?"

He was teasing her, but testing, too. "What book did you have in mind?" she asked.

"Uh . . . *Fifty Word Games*, the book you gave me when you came to visit."

"Did you have a chance to look at it?"

"Just a little. Diane flipped through it for me. I used to like that stuff, though, when I was a kid."

"How about now?"

"Yeah. Now, too, I guess. Haven't thought about it much. Try me on one."

"I will before I leave," she said. "Now I'm going to give you a couple of *Crime and Punishment* questions. You're to answer them orally the next time. I'm purposely not going to write the questions for you. Part of the point is to memorize them, to build up your memory power. Ready for number one? What makes Raskolnikov think he's extraordinary—a special person who can do no wrong? Got that? Number two: After the murders, what signs are there that Raskolnikov is plagued by guilt? O.K.? Remember key words. Number three—"

"Ms. Treer?" His eyes darted around the room. "Did you ever have a hallucination?"

"Not really. Why?"

"Nothing. No reason. I was thinking about Raskolnikov."

"Good. We'll talk about his mental state next time. Now, number three: What indications do we have that Raskolnikov wants the truth to be revealed, that he wants to be punished?"

Gary closed his eyes, grimaced.

"What? What are you thinking?"

"About truth," he said.

"That's a big subject." She paused. "What about it?"

"Whether there is such a thing. Whether anybody really tells it."

"What do you think?" she asked.

"I think . . . people don't tell the truth."

"What makes you say that?"

"Because nobody I know does, not all the time, anyway."

"Maybe you haven't met enough people yet."

"Maybe." Gary stared at the wall. "Do you think people can be trusted?" he asked.

Who was he thinking of—Diane? "I don't know about most people," Ann said, "but I've been lucky enough to know a few who've been completely trustworthy."

Gary was silent.

Ann cleared her throat. "I'm going in a couple of minutes, Gary, so let's make sure you know what your responsibilities are for next time, O.K.?"

"Yeah."

"Read two chapters. Is that fair? Prepare the three oral questions, and dictate a page a day to Diane for the journal. I'll arrange it with her."

"O.K."

"Now," she said, "ready for the big challenge?"

"What?"

"Word games—remember?"

"Oh, yeah. Go ahead."

"You know how to play anagrams, right? Rearranging letters to make a different word? Well, by the time I come again, think of an anagram for your name. If possible, one that says something about you."

"What do you mean?"

"Take ADOLF HITLER, for example. You can rearrange the letters and get HATED FOR ILL. Or FLORENCE NIGHTINGALE —FLIT ON, CHEERING ANGEL!

"Did you make those up?"

"No, I got them out of your book, but I made up one for my own name—Ann U. Treer—U for my maiden name, Unger. You're allowed to use your middle initial. Mine's hard because of the three double letters in such a short name."

"Come on, stop making excuses. What is it?"

"Mine doesn't describe me, unless I start selling pot as a sideline."

"What is it?"

"Ann U. Treer rearranged—TEA RUNNER. Or another one: NEARER NUT. You can probably do better than that with your name. What's your middle initial?"

"G, for George."

"O.K. Think of one for next time. That'll keep you busy when you're not reading *Crime and Punishment.*"

"Yeah."

She put her hand on the frame, brushed against Gary's arm. "I'm going now. I'll be seeing you Friday this week." She took her coat off the hook. "Any message for Diane?"

He didn't answer.

"Gary?"

"Could I trust you?" he asked suddenly in a low voice.

She looked at him, surprised. "Yes—"

"Would you do me a favor?"

"If I can."

"Bring me a couple of books from the library?"

"Sure," she said, relieved. "Which ones?"

"Books—that I could read—that we could read when you're here."

"O.K. What books?"

"Books about what's wrong with me. You know, about spine injuries."

She tried to keep the tone of her voice even. "Wouldn't your doctor have access to those, I mean, to better ones than I could get?"

"I guess so. Forget it then."

Ann shifted her weight to the other foot. "Can you ask him?"

"Sure. Yeah. I'll ask him."

Gary was staring at the wall now. Ann watched him. Their eyes met. She rested her coat on the edge of the frame. "Do you prefer . . . that the books come from the library?"

"Yes," he said quickly.

"And that I take them with me when I leave here?"

"Yes."

"You don't want to ask anyone else, then?"

"No."

Why was on her tongue, but she didn't say it. Why not ask the doctor? Your parents? Something told her, though, that *why* at this moment would scare him back into hiding. "I'll do what I can," she said. "You mustn't count on me, though. I don't know what books I can get."

Gary smiled ironically. "Just get one that widens my view of the world."

"So you do see the value of books!" Ann said.

"Yeah. They tell us about ourselves."

Ann put on her coat slowly. "Good-bye," she said. "Remember the homework." She turned to go. "And the anagram."

"Yeah. So long. Don't get caught."

"Caught?"

"Tea Runner."

Ann hurried into the corridor toward the elevator. So Gary knew. It was evident in his expression, in his eyes. And he'd chosen her to be his agent in confirming it. Why her? Because she wasn't as likely to judge him as the doctor was, probably. Not about to measure his manhood as his friends might. Because she hadn't borne him, with all the pain and expectations surrounding that. Because she didn't worship him and hanker for him, as Diane did. Because she was only his teacher. Still, as such, a privileged person who could get away with bringing up high-sounding subjects that other people avoided, like guilt and truth.

Ann went down in the elevator. She had to talk to somebody about this—the doctor, somebody. Even if she knew what books Gary wanted, sneaking them in was absurd. On the other hand, Gary had asked for her trust, and she had said yes. She wouldn't go back on that. Doctors were notoriously hard to locate, but she'd heard Mrs. Madden say that he was back from a convention. Ann got out of the elevator on the ground floor and looked up and down the roster of physicians. Kimball, she saw, had an office in Room 102.

chapter 7

Gary closed his eyes, pictured GARY G. MADDEN written in white on a clean chalkboard. As a kid he had studied for spelling tests by imagining how the words looked on a chalkboard. Now he needed an anagram that described him. MADMAN? Nope, he was short one M right from the start. GAY MAN? Hell, no, not him—not in any sense of that word—plus the leftover letters, *RGDDE*, were useless. What a stupid way to be passing time, but you had to do something to keep from going crazy while you were alone. His mother had come up since Treer left, but she'd gone out again to make a phone call. Tommy, the only other person around, was still zonked from his medication.

Would Treer really bring him those books? he wondered. He couldn't stop thinking about it. It had been pretty shrewd of him to ask her. A serious person like her, always rapping about books being so important. And saying that people were trustworthy. O.K., let her prove it. Too bad he had to drag her into this, but it was the way that would cause the least shake-up. Just like learning about sex. If you wanted the story straight, without everybody turning red in the face, get it out of a book. O.K., today was Wednesday. Treer would probably have something for him Friday when she came again. Two more days to wait. Until then, he swore he'd keep his mind off the subject. Stick with anagrams. Jesus, he *was* going nuts or he wouldn't be lying here playing a word game.

Gary opened his eyes and made the chalkboard disappear. It was so cool to be able to picture something in your mind and then make it come and go. Too bad you couldn't control real life that way. Anything was possible in your head, though. Shut your eyes, for instance, and picture Diane. Hair like silk. What the hell did silk look like? Anyway, pale gold hair, slightly darker underneath. She put something on it to make the top blonder. But it didn't make her look cheap. She *couldn't* look cheap. No way. And then her eyes—very dark blue. Longish neck. Swanlike? Well, that was exaggerating. And her body—rounded, full. Definitely not fat. But soft when his arms were around her. Like in her house that night toward the end of summer, when they'd come back from the shore and her parents weren't home yet. . . . The two of them, still in bathing suits, lying on the living-room floor, feeling the nubby carpet under them. "When will they be home?" he'd whispered. "Soon!" Still, she had let him turn out the light. Oh, man, that was the closest they had come. . . . Come. Ha, not quite. Damn it.

"Get off my back!"

Gary opened his eyes. Tommy was raving in his sleep again. He'd been doing that off and on—sleeping, raving, then waking up and going on a kind of talking jag. What a weirdo. "A nice young man," Gary's mother had said the day Tommy came. Since then she'd been superpolite to him, which showed how she'd changed her mind. Gary looked in the direction of the other bed, but he couldn't see much. He wished Tommy would wake up. He could use a little conversation.

Of course what he ought to be doing as soon as his mother came back was reading *Crime and Punishment*. Treer probably wouldn't even show him a medical book on Friday until he'd done his regular assignments. He was just at the part now where Raskolnikov was returning to the scene of his crime. Stupid jerk. Or was he? Couldn't help it, probably, just like he himself kept returning, even though he didn't want to, to that second-half kickoff against the Bears. The high end-over-end kick. Cleats digging up turf as he zeroed in. Billy alongside him at first, yelling something. Dodging the Bears' number 10. Suddenly, closer than he'd thought, Lionetti with the ball—the tackle—*zing*.

Why? That was the thing, *why?* Sheer bad luck? A punishment for something he'd done—or *hadn't* done? That's the way some people thought God reffed the game. O.K., then, if this was the punishment, how long was it for? And *what was the crime?*

"Hey, Sister Marie. . . ?"

Gary listened. Tommy was coming around. "Tommy?" Gary said. "You awake?"

"Hell, yeah. I been awake. What is it, day or night?" He coughed.

"Afternoon," Gary said. "Almost suppertime."

"For *you*, buddy. I'm still getting mine piped in around the clock, remember?"

"Yeah. Tasty?"

"Uh, could use a little more seasoning, you know. Too bad, too, because I think it's a liquid jumbo taco they're running through me." Tommy coughed again, caught his breath. "So what's been going down?"

"Not much," Gary said. "How do you feel?"

"Don't ask. I got these electric knives slicing me whenever I move."

"Even after the pain-killer?"

"Well, it don't exactly kill the pain. It just sort of beats on it and leaves it lying there half dead."

"Can you ask for more pills?"

"I could *ask*, man, but I wouldn't *get*. What I need is a little help from my friends. I mean, I need what this buddy of mine has—a little something besides what the doctor orders."

"Could you get away with that?"

"Who's to know? My old lady ain't here to keep an eye on me."

"Where is she—your mother? Wasn't she here?"

"Yeah, well, Friday she flew in, you know, and stayed til Tuesday. First time I seen her in a while. She had to get back to Florida, to her husband. She's remarried. If I'm lucky she'll get my old man to foot some of the medical bills. Where's your mom today? Still holding the fort?"

"Yeah. She went to call one of my teachers."

"What for?"

"This Mrs. Purdy didn't show up when she was supposed to."

"I forgot you're a schoolboy. Teachers gonna come up, and all that shit?"

"Yeah. My English teacher was here just now."

"English teacher. An old bag?"

"No, young."

"Anything like Dottie?"

"No, nothing like her. Nice-looking, though."

"Wake me up next time she comes."

"I will," Gary said. "Hey, how come you quit school?"

"I wasn't getting nothing out of it."

"Isn't working rough?"

"Not bad. I mean, I'm into this landscaping. Get a lot of time off in winter. It ain't bad. I like it. When they pull rank on me around this place, I tell them, 'Watch who you're talking to, man, I'm a tree surgeon myself.' "

Gary smiled. "I'd like to send Kimball off to be a tree surgeon."

"Your doctor giving you the business?"

"How do you mean, the business?"

"Holding out on telling you what's what?"

"Yeah, that's exactly what he's doing."

"Listen, buddy, they *always* do that. You know why?"

"Why?"

"Because those guys can't stand being wrong. Say nothing and you can't be wrong, right?"

"I guess so. Hell, if I were a doctor, I'd give a person all the dope."

"Dig it. So would I. But these glory boys play it safe— wait until you're better, then tell you what it was you *had*, and expect you to kiss their asses for curing you."

"Maybe. All doctors couldn't be the same."

Tommy sighed. "They are, believe me, and I should know. I've seen enough of 'em."

"How many?"

"Doctors? I lost count. Four, no, five hospitals—since I was fourteen."

"For what?"

"Once appendicitis, the rest—accidents. A power mower, a minibike, and twice with a motorcycle."

"You must feel like somebody's got it in for you," Gary said.

"Hell, no. Chance."

"Not carelessness?"

"No way. I like to go fast, see, but speed alone don't get you. You can be winging along at a hundred fifty and you'll be all right as long as there's no rock or something on the road."

"And you don't think anybody—I mean, some higher being or something—puts the rock on the road?"

"What're you, kidding me? What do you think, there's a guy with a long white beard spreading rocks around for certain people?"

"You know what I mean," Gary said. "Don't you ever think back to that rock that got you, and wonder how it happened to get there?"

"Hell, no. What would it prove?"

"That there was a cause."

"You're full of shit," Tommy said. "It *happened,* that's all."

"But why to you, or to me, instead of to somebody else?"

"Buddy, you're gonna mess up your head with all that heavy stuff. Too many books, man! Send the teachers back to school. Put on the TV. You got a stereo?"

"At home."

"Tell your mother to go get it."

"It's not portable."

"That wouldn't stop your old lady."

"Probably not," Gary said. Maybe Tommy was right—he *was* gonna mess up his head by thinking too much. NEARER NUT. He was nearer to being a nut than Treer was. He pictured the chalkboard again. GARY G. MADDEN. MAD. NAG. DARN. DAMN! All of them in his name, but still no terrific anagram.

"No offense, huh?" Tommy's foghorn voice blared. "I mean about your mother and the stereo. I meant that friendly. I'd never snap on a buddy's mother."

"Offense?" Gary said. "Are you kidding? Forget it. Hey, Tommy, ever hear of Phillips Institute?"

"Hear of it? I'm going there. In three, four weeks. You going, too?"

"Yeah."

"How about that. Well, I never been there myself, you know, but I have a friend spent six months in the place. It's out in the country. Good therapists. I mean good-looking. Food, so-so. Strict rules—no booze or dope. Unless you're smart enough."

"What about the doctors? Are they good?"

"The best, man. My buddy walked out of there. Took him six months, but he walked out. You should meet this cat. He was in a head-on collision on the parkway. Both cars caught fire. My buddy got out just before the gas tank exploded. The driver of the other car couldn't get out. The cops had to wait until the fire died down before they could even look. And then, guess what they saw."

"What?"

"It was grisly, man. The driver was sitting at the wheel, I mean, just like he was cruising along. Except for one thing. He was completely charred—a cinder. And when the cop touched the guy, his head fell off. One big ash. What a way to go, huh?"

"Come on," Gary said. "You're putting me on."

"No, man!"

"How do you know all those details?" Gary asked.

"My buddy told me."

"He was conscious?"

"Yeah," Tommy said. "You were conscious, weren't you, when they carried you off the field?"

"Sure, but everything was a blur." He tried to remember how it had been. On his back on a board, helmet still in place, people bending over him. Applause. The band playing a salute, or had he imagined that? Diane running alongside as they carried him to the ambulance. His mother's face on the way to the hospital—her lipstick smeared. "I doubt your friend would know all the details," he said to Tommy.

"Are you kidding? This guy has a sensational memory. He's a lucky S.O.B. altogether. Just missed getting blown sky high, and now he's completely cemented together. They did that at Phillips. He's already working again. Yeah, they fix you up good there," Tommy said. "Unless you got *real* bad luck. Like this one dude my buddy knew."

"What happened to him?"

"Well, the guy was a quad—you know, a quadriplegic. He'd been doing gymnastics. Fell off a trampoline and landed on his head. He got his cord severed—not just injured like us. Couldn't move his arms or legs at all, poor sonofabitch. Couldn't do nothing. Finally, after a hell of a long time, they got him so he could be propped up in a wheelchair. The only way the poor dude could make it move, though, was to blow through a sort of a little pipe.

A breath-powered wheelchair, how do you like that?"

Gary felt his throat tightening. The ceiling seemed to be getting wavy.

"Well," Tommy went on, "this guy got a big kick out of blowing himself around in the chair. I mean, he was pretty cheerful, my buddy said, a pretty good sport. He had a good-looking wife, this guy, and she used to come get him on weekends sometimes and take him home. Well, one weekend he went home and—"

"Tommy, hey, can you hold the story?" Gary said. "Can you press the button for the nurse? I need a . . . drink. I need something. . . ."

"Sure. Ouch." Tommy slid his arm toward the button. "Hey, something wrong, man?"

"I'm not sure. Don't mind me. I'm tired from talking. Just gonna close my eyes, O.K.?"

"O.K. by me. You're thinking too much, kid. That's your problem. Get your old lady to bring up that stereo."

Sister Marie answered the call, and then his mother came back. Before long the orderlies flipped him, the aide brought the dinner tray, and when his father appeared, he read from the newspaper. Somebody put on TV, and Tommy, after his medication, fell asleep again. Everything was O.K., Gary kept telling himself. Everything was under control. But he knew he was lying. He had sworn to himself that he wouldn't think about important things, at least until Friday. But now his mind, along with his body, was refusing to take orders. During the evening everybody had wanted to know why he was so quiet, but he hadn't answered. And at bedtime he surprised the nurse by asking for a sleeping pill. Since she couldn't get any without the doctor's permission, he had lain awake for a long time.

He dozed off at last, and in his dream he was home, at

his house, and Ms. Treer was there. She was challenging him to turn the pages of a thick book by blowing on them, but it was hard, and he couldn't do it. And when the orderlies came at half past midnight to turn him onto his back, he woke up with a jolt and realized that his eyes were wet from crying.

chapter 8

O.K., she'd do it, Ann thought. She climbed out of the water and dried herself off. She couldn't tutor Gary on Friday until she'd consulted his parents. Kimball had agreed. So call the Maddens. Get it over with. Still in her swimsuit, she looked up the number and put a coin in the locker-room telephone. Holding one hand against her ear to filter out the confusion of voices and the clanking of locker doors, she listened to the telephone ringing.

"Hello?"

"Hello, Mrs. Madden?"

"Yes."

"This is Ann Treer, Gary's teacher." She paused.

"Oh, yes, Mrs. Treer . . ."

"I'm sorry to bother you, but I'm at my health club right now—not too far from you—and there's something I'd like to speak to you about concerning Gary's tutoring—"

"Is something wrong, Mrs. Treer?"

"Not exactly. I saw Dr. Kimball this afternoon, and he thought it would be a good idea if I—consulted you." She took a breath. "Is there any possibility I could drop by for a minute right now? I'm not far from your house. Would that be too inconvenient?"

"Why—no. Not at all."

"Fine, then I'll be there as soon as I can. Just for a few minutes. Wilmot Terrace, number eighteen—right?"

"Yes, that's it."

"Thank you. I'll be right over."

Ignoring the din of the locker room, she dressed quickly and threw her suit into the gym bag. What was she, a masochist, stopping off on a cold night, tired, her hair damp, to bring up a delicate subject with a pair of stricken parents?

Ann left the club and headed toward Wilmot Terrace. A good person, Dr. Kimball, she thought as she drove slowly, looking in the dark at the names on dimly lit street signs. It had been a stroke of luck in the first place to find him at the hospital. She'd been prepared for total elusiveness, a quick brushoff, or an ego trip, but the man had been available, concerned, and cordial. What if Gary asked her questions about his condition? "Let's get this settled today," Kimball had said. The Maddens had asked him to wait to tell Gary the whole story, but if Gary was asking questions, he ought to be getting answers. He'd speak to the Maddens immediately. Ann should see them, too, he suggested, on behalf of the tutors.

But did she really need to get herself into this? she

thought as she turned onto Wilmot Terrace. She could, after all, just go to the hospital Friday and tell Gary to concentrate on schoolwork. She might be better off altogether sticking strictly to business. Business—ridiculous. Gary wasn't *business*. There he was on that frame, as alone and frightened as the character in Kafka's *The Metamorphosis*, who wakes up one morning and finds himself transformed into a giant insect. She'd had a touch of that feeling herself after Mike's death. *She* hadn't changed, but her position had. Friends, even the most sympathetic and well-intentioned, had put her, as a new widow, in a special category, a kind of untouchable caste, when all she wanted was to be treated like everyone else.

Ann slowed down and looked for the house number. The street was what she had expected: pleasant, modest, middle-class. Combination brick and frame houses; lots of shrubbery. A porch light on at number 18. They were expecting her. She parked the car, walked up the path to the porch, and rang the doorbell. As she stood waiting, she felt a quick current of self-consciousness run through her.

The door opened a crack. "Mrs. Treer?"

"Yes."

Mrs. Madden let her in. "How are you this evening? Chilly out there tonight, isn't it? Please come in."

"Yes, it is chilly." Ann shivered, damp hair clinging to the back of her neck.

"Hello." Mr. Madden appeared in the doorway to the living room. "I'm Gary's father. I don't believe we've met."

"Hello. I'm Ann Treer," she said. Like Gary in facial structure, she noticed. More bland, though. Early forties, probably. "How's Gary tonight?" she asked him.

Mr. Madden hesitated.

"Oh, he was fine," Mrs. Madden said. "He read a little

Crime and Punishment when he was on his stomach. I turned the pages for him. He complains about that book, Mrs. Treer! Won't you come into the living room?" she asked.

"Yes, thank you."

Mr. Madden ushered her to the couch, hastily pulled a newspaper out of the way.

"Please sit down," Mrs. Madden said. "You'll forgive us if things are a little—out of order around here? We just got home from the hospital before you telephoned."

"Oh, I'm sorry. Then you haven't had dinner?"

"Oh, yes. Yes, we have," Mrs. Madden said. "We had something to eat over there."

The three of them sat down awkwardly.

"Hank," Mrs. Madden said, "this is the young woman who came all the way back last Friday to deliver a note to Gary."

"Oh, yes." He nodded. "Gary appreciated that. My wife tells me you've been the soul of patience."

"She's been setting a great example for all of us," Ann said. She glanced around the room. Ordinary, not unlike her own parents' house. Scrupulously neat, in spite of the apology. Slipcovered couch. Blond coffee table. Beige rug. Fireplace that looked unused. Painted portrait of Gary over the mantelpiece. "I like that painting," Ann said.

"Yes, isn't that good?" Mrs. Madden reached for an envelope on the coffee table. "And these just came today. Gary's yearbook proofs." She showed them to Ann.

"I can hardly recognize him with a jacket and tie," Mr. Madden said. "You must know how these kids are about dressing up."

"Yes, well," Mrs. Madden said, "that day I didn't have to beg him. He's always looked forward to being a senior, working on that yearbook. . . . He's sports editor, you know."

"Yes." Ann watched Mr. Madden, who was clenching and unclenching his fists.

"Do you think they'll assign that job to somebody else?" Mr. Madden asked his wife.

"Well, I guess so," she said. "Gary won't be back to school for—"

"You must be wondering why I called," Ann said, groping for an opening. "Mrs. Madden," she said, "before I came down to get you in the coffee shop this afternoon, I spoke to Dr. Kimball. He told me he'd try to see you. Did he have a chance?"

"Yes, briefly," Mrs. Madden said warily.

She wasn't going to get any help on this, Ann saw. She'd have to take the plunge. "Well, I've got a problem about tutoring Gary, and I thought maybe you could advise me."

"Are the lessons going to take too much of your time?" Mrs. Madden asked.

"No, it's not that kind of problem." Ann began slowly. "I found myself in a difficult position today. I sensed that Gary was very preoccupied, very worried. I don't know if you'll think this is my business or not, but I believe it is, because his schoolwork won't be worth anything until he can concentrate." She paused.

"Do you mean Gary's not ready for schoolwork yet?" Mr. Madden asked. "Don't you think the work'll help him keep his mind off the illness?"

"He probably is ready—physically," Ann said. "I think though—I don't know—today I was afraid he was on the brink of asking me questions I couldn't answer, and I wish the person with the answers could give them to Gary before something upsetting happens. I think he's crying out to us for more information about what's wrong with him."

The room was quiet, as if the Maddens were waiting to hear the cry.

"There are different ways to handle situations like this. We know that," Mrs. Madden said. Her voice was high-pitched now. "Some people swear by that famous hospital where they tell the patient the most awful things the very same night. To me that's cruel."

"Dr. Kimball gave us an opinion after three days," Mr. Madden said. "He felt it was too indefinite before that even for us, as the parents. And as for Gary, well, we've been waiting for just the right time to tell him how serious this thing is."

"Isn't it possible," Ann said quietly, "that he already suspects and that the hush-hush is scaring him?"

"It's possible. . . ." Mr. Madden said.

Mrs. Madden nervously rubbed her neck and stared at an invisible focal point on the rug. "I don't think he realizes," she said. "Of course he's not acting like his normal self. He's a very sick boy. But he expects a complete recovery, I know he does—and I want him to think like that. A person needs hope." She looked to her husband for agreement. "In our family, we've always found that hope in the church," she said, "in believing in God and an afterlife. Everything I do, I do because of that hope. I think Gary will work at getting better if he sees hope. If he sees none," her voice broke, "then what will become of him?"

Ann cleared her throat. "I don't think Dr. Kimball would ever rule out hope, would he, no matter what he said to Gary?"

"Well, I suppose Dr. Kimball thinks he knows what's

best for Gary," Mrs. Madden said, "but how can he know better than a mother knows—better than his father and I know? Why, I remember the day we brought Gary home as a baby to this house. We had just moved in. Hank painted his room while I was in the hospital. That's the only time until now that Gary's ever stayed in a hospital. He was such a good baby when I washed him and changed him and fed him. He hardly cried for anything. . . ."

Ann glanced from one of them to the other. She'd once been a lot like them in thinking of her safe, ordinary past as a charm to ward off tragedy.

"And I stayed home all those years to be with him," Mrs. Madden went on, "because—well—we knew there wouldn't be any others—and of course in those days there weren't chances for women like there are now. So I spent my life here in this house, but I never regretted it, not one bit," she said vehemently. "And when he wanted to play this football, and his father was all for it, I thought, well, that's what he wants to do, so"—her face was lined with tension now—"so I *know* my son. I know how much these sports and activities mean to him, and then I look at that empty bed upstairs and I think, how can I let Gary believe that *that's* going to be his life—lying in that bed?"

"But the limits would never be that narrow," Ann said. She looked at the Maddens hesitantly. "Dr. Kimball says that Gary'll continue to get back movement and feeling for a year, maybe even longer." They were urging her on. "And with hard work he can get back the use of his arms." She was repeating what Kimball must have told them already, but maybe repetition was what they needed. "And the best thing," Ann said, "is that Gary's mind is absolutely intact. Isn't that what really matters? I believe I'm speaking for the other tutors, too. I'm not trying to give you advice, but

I think we can keep his mind challenged better, once he knows the truth."

"You're making it sound so easy to tell him," Mrs. Madden said.

"I'm the last one to think it's going to be easy," Ann said. "I've recently come away from a great hurt myself, and I know that in things like this nothing's easy."

"Of course," Mrs. Madden said. "Yes. I heard about your loss, and I'm so sorry."

"What's helped me a little," Ann pressed on, passing up sympathy, "has been trying to face up to it."

Mr. Madden coughed.

"You think Dr. Kimball should tell Gary the next time he sees him," Mrs. Madden said. "You want him to put it the way he did with me this afternoon, to tell Gary that— *the paralysis is permanent. That he'll never walk?*" She sat stiffly, hearing the reverberations of her own words.

Mr. Madden was shielding his eyes with his hand.

Ann, sitting very still, gave them the silence they needed. This was the first time, obviously, that those words had been spoken in this house. Suddenly she remembered something Dr. Kimball had said. *The family is always sick along with the patient. . . .* That was the case here. The Maddens were still in shock. They'd undergone their own metamorphosis, just as she had with Mike's death, and here they were—sufferers without the luxury of sickbeds. She thought she understood now why they were keeping Gary in limbo. It was the parents who hadn't been ready for the truth.

But now it was out. Even though she hadn't intended to, Mrs. Madden had spoken it, and it had penetrated. Ann watched them—Mrs. Madden, her lips pressed together tightly in despair; Mr. Madden, getting up and putting his hands on his wife's shoulders, a gesture affecting in its clumsiness.

"She's right, Helen. He has to be told."

Mrs. Madden nodded. "The next time Dr. Kimball sees him is Friday morning."

There weren't going to be any tears, Ann saw. She wished there would be, but monitoring feelings and keeping self-control were essential to the Madden code. "So he'll know by the time I see him," Ann said. She rose from the couch. "Should I keep on schedule then?" she asked. "Should I tutor him Friday?"

Mrs. Madden gently lifted her husband's hands from her shoulders and stood up. "Yes, Mrs. Treer. Please."

Mrs. Madden was reorganizing herself, Ann realized, was looking for enough room to fit the truth in between hope and the Madden code.

"It was awfully good of you to come by," Mrs. Madden said as she saw Ann to the door. Mr. Madden opened it to the night air, and Ann stepped onto the porch. "Once again," Mrs. Madden called to her as she walked down the path, "we certainly appreciate all you're doing, and so does Gary!"

It was almost the same Mrs. Madden speaking, Ann thought—almost.

chapter

T-Day. If he ever wrote his autobiography, Gary decided, that's what he'd call it. Friday, October 8—Truth Day, the beginning of his new life, as Kimball had said. He lay on his stomach with the copy of *Crime and Punishment* under his frame. Not that he'd gotten past the first sentence on the page. He couldn't believe they'd finally left him alone after all the action in the morning. The TV was turned off. Tommy was out for tests, and his mother had actually gone down for a cup of coffee. A good stiff shot of something was what she needed. Instead they had given *him* the tranquilizer. Around here, T-Day meant Tranquilizer Day. At St. Agnes, if anybody was in danger of facing the truth, *Dope them up* was the motto. That was one thing that annoyed him. The other thing was Kimball's asking him if he wanted to talk to the staff psychologist. What did they think, that he couldn't handle hearing that he'd probably never walk?

Hell, he'd been way down for a couple of days because he *wanted* the goddam truth. Nothing was more crazy-making than the business he'd been getting with the whispers and the stories of quads in breath-powered wheelchairs. Now that he'd heard the worst from Kimball, all he could say was, what a relief!

Not that he'd been expecting it when he got it. Nothing was going according to schedule on this freaked-out day, he thought, as he flicked his wrist up and down on the extension attached to his frame. First of all, he'd awakened from a miserable sleep and held daily tryouts for his muscles. Except this time—success. He'd extended his right wrist! Not anywhere near the normal extension, but *movement*. His arm was coming back! His *right* arm. So he'd just been bragging a little to Tommy about what an ace pitcher he'd been as a kid, when Kimball had suddenly appeared at eight A.M. His parents were out in the waiting room, Kimball had told him. His father at eight in the morning? He had to admit it, his head had started swimming. Kimball had even pulled the gruesome green curtains around the bed.

"Waited to catch you on a good day," Kimball had said with a half smile. "Go on, do your stuff."

Gary had extended his wrist.

"Very good. Still tension of the radial extensors, but . . ."

Come on, Kimball, get on with it. "How come my father's out there?" he had asked.

"To pin a medal on you for being the best patient on the floor." Kimball had put his hand on Gary's upper arm, where he had sensation. "Look, Gary, I have a couple of things to tell you now that you're coming along so well."

Businesslike but sincere. Go ahead.

"First the worst, and all uphill afterward, fair enough?"

"Yeah," Gary said. Kimball was looking him straight in the eye. He appreciated that.

"I want you to begin preparing today for a new life—for the life of a man who in all probability won't be able to walk," Kimball said. "Now every once in a while there's a doctor in this world who makes a wrong prediction, and in this case, I'd love for it to be me. But on the basis of my knowledge and experience, I say you've got to prepare yourself not to walk. We've got to be realistic. It's next to impossible." Kimball raised his eyebrows. "Watch it now. I'm not saying 'Think crippled.' See if you get the difference. I'm saying, begin today to work on all the things you're going to need *twice as badly,* if you aren't walking. Then, if you were to get really lucky, you'd just be a little overprepared. See what I mean? Work on getting the muscles back in your upper extremities. Cooperate with diet and drinking liquids so you're in good shape internally. And the main thing—work on your head. Know what I mean by that?"

"What?"

"Your head—your attitude—is going to make or break you. They say doctors think they're gods. That may be true of some, but I'm saying, do you know who's going to make a bigger difference in your comeback than I am? Or than any doctor at Phillips Institute?"

"Yeah."

"Who?"

"Me."

Kimball smiled. "How did you know?"

87

"You ever been a coach?"

"It's the same principle. When it comes to football, I'm only an armchair coach, but some of the same thinking applies in rehabilitation. Now, a key point," Kimball went on. "Remember I started out saying 'Think of yourself as a *man* who—' "

"Yeah."

"I said *man*. Whether or not you're one of the luckiest ones in your rehabilitation, *you can still lead a full life.* Your luck is holding out so far—you've had no complications, no skin breakdown. You're getting muscles back. Your insurance is covering medical expenses. You have terrific, supportive parents and friends behind you. You're going to have the best rehabilitation available. I know of dozens of men and women, some with higher lesions than yours, who lead happy, productive lives. They go to college, they work, they go on vacations, some of them get married. If you work on mind and body, you can be one of them."

"I'll try."

Kimball leaned over and pressed his arm again. "I think you will. I'm only an armchair coach, but I can usually pick a winner. And you know, you'll be out of these tongs in another couple of weeks. That'll make a big difference in your slant on things."

"Yeah. This slant stinks."

"You're right, and that reminds me of another important thing. You're going to have a lot of ups and downs throughout this thing. The downs are going to hit you hard. I suggest you talk your feelings out with somebody. Right from the start. Don't wait until you hit a low. How would you like to talk to the staff psychologist?"

No thanks. What kind of patients were they used to around here—loonies? Screaming meemies? Hell, his head already *was* together, Gary thought. Who needed a Pastor Shafer or a staff psychologist?

T-Day. What had he thought about in those first few minutes after Kimball left? Mostly he'd felt a big urge to get going with the work. He'd felt like pulling out the tongs the way he had in his dream, felt like standing up—just to prove Kimball wrong on the spot. He'd cool it, though. He wasn't dumb enough to expect magic. He'd do it their way, working a little at a time.

Then his parents had come in. Weird scene. Not sad or emotional. Just shyness all around. Something like the night he'd almost made it with Diane and had come home to find his parents waiting up for him. This morning his father had come close to the frame, had almost touched him. "We'll show them, Gary," his mother had said.

So here he was now, supposedly reading *Crime and Punishment*, though he couldn't get far until his mother came back to turn pages. Treer'd be up in a little while. Too bad he'd put her to that trouble about bringing books. And—oh, hell—the anagram! Well, he'd better do school-work first, the important stuff. How was he going to make a comeback and become President, like FDR, unless he got smart? He focused his eyes on the page below him, under the frame. He didn't believe it. The fourth sentence on the page: "*A normal man, it is true, hardly exists,*" he read. "*Among dozens—perhaps hundreds of thousands—hardly one is to be met with.*" So, great. He had plenty of company.

"Hey, Gary . . ."

Must be hearing things. Call the shrink after all. Somebody whispering his name?

"Gary. . . . Hey, don't strain, man. I'm coming to *you*. Hey!"

"Jason! I'll be damned."

Jason pushed aside the book and table and lay flat on his back on the floor so that Gary could see his face as he looked through the opening in the frame.

"Jesus, you look silly down there. What time is it?" Gary asked. "Don't you have a class?"

"It's last period," Jason whispered. "Now what kind of horse's ass would I be if I couldn't cut a class to see a sick buddy?"

"You cut?"

"Getting out of there was nothing compared to getting in here," Jason said. "Those sisters sure keep tight security. They'll never see me under here, though." He lay back and put his hands behind his head. "So what's happening?"

"It's T-Day," Gary said.

"T-Day?"

"T for truth. The doctor told me something this morning. Says I'm probably not going to walk."

Jason's face froze. He pulled his hands from behind his head, covered his eyes, and uncovered them slowly. "Man, that's gonna be a hard road."

"Yeah."

Jason kept staring up at him. "How you gonna deal with that?"

"I'm not gonna take it sitting down," Gary said, uncertain whether he was laughing or crying.

Jason, smiling, shook his head. "I think you're gonna beat this thing, buddy, you know?" he said faintly. "If anybody can, you can. Know why I say that? 'Cause you can laugh."

"Seeing you down there on your ass would make anybody laugh."

Jason sat up so that his face was close to Gary's. "Man, you can laugh at me til the nuns come and call a bust. I mean, anything I can *do—anything—*and not just on T-Day—"

"Thanks," Gary said. Neither of them spoke for a few seconds. "So how's everybody?" Gary went on in a rush. "You up for the game this Saturday?"

"Up as I'll ever be."

"Good. So football's out for me. That's a bummer."

"Never mind," Jason said. "Leave the game to us goons. You're retiring a hero."

"Yeah. A George Gipp."

"Pick another one. Not him."

"Why?"

"First, 'cause he's dead. Don't be a dead hero, man. Second, no offense to the guy personally, but I don't like it when they turn some poor raggedy jock into a saint. Like Gipp, like Lombardi."

"They were good guys, right?"

"Hell, good as you and me. Good at playing or coaching football. But all this inspiration, loyal sons of this and that —that's a crock. Know the truth about George Gipp?"

"What?"

"He left Notre Dame to play for money at another school. They had to drag him back. And you know how he died at such a young age? He went on a five-day binge and caught pneumonia."

"You're putting me on."

"I read it in a book."

"What've you got on Lombardi?"

"Nixon was thinking of putting him on his ticket as Vice President."

"Come off it."

"I'm serious." Jason stretched. "Goddam, this floor's hard. When they going to turn you?"

"Soon."

"The point is—hey, Gary, look at me, man."

He looked at Jason.

"The point is, don't try to be a saint. O.K.? Promise? Yell when it hurts, O.K.?"

"What kind of a coach would *you* be!"

"No Lombardi, that's for sure. You win for *you*, man, O.K.?"

"Gary, how're you doing?"

He heard his mother's footsteps.

"Sister Marie *made* me take this long break. Mrs. Treer is here, dear, and the orderlies are going to turn you. Oh!" his mother said, "I didn't know anyone was here."

Jason crawled out from under the frame. "Just paying a little visit, Mrs. Madden. I'll be leaving now. Football practice."

"Oh."

Jason slung his arm around Gary's shoulders and whispered in his ear. "Pick another hero, O.K.? Not the Gipper."

"All right. See you, Jay." Was Jason grabbing his hand? Yeah, he was. "Thanks for coming, Jay."

"They're ready to turn you, Gary," his mother repeated.

The orderlies prepared him and did their job. Turning not quite as bad, now that he knew there were only a couple more weeks to go. Heave-ho. Face up.

"Mrs. Treer's waiting," his mother said. "I think she prefers if I wait in the lounge."

Treer. He'd have to fake it with *Crime and Punishment*. Maybe he could get her to discuss the idea that a normal man hardly exists. Or get her to read his journal right away. Or stall her with anagrams. GARY G. MADDEN. Picture a chalk-board . . . DAMN . . . GARY G. DE left over. Hey, what was that Jason had said about poor jocks? Oh, man, terrific!

"Hi, Gary."

Treer was standing by the frame.

"How are you?" she asked.

"Good. A weird day."

"I brought you some books."

"Good. Hey, Ms. Treer, I've got my anagram."

"What is it?"

She was looking—softer than usual. Was it his tran-quilizer? "GARY G. MADDEN rearranged," he said, "DAMN RAGGEDY. Maybe for now, Ms. Treer. But just you wait."

chapter 10

"Hey, Gary . . ."

"Yeah?" Treer had just left. T-Day lesson over. Gary saw in the mirror that Tommy, back from his tests, was propping himself up on one elbow.

"She's a *teacher?*"

"Yeah. Is this the first time you saw her?"

"First time she's been here that I wasn't strung out. Not bad, not bad." Tommy, beginning to cough, lay back. "What do you say you learn from that broad?"

"English."

"English? Hell, I knew that since I was born. What's all this boop-de-doo I heard, about confessions and love and all that jazz—that's English?"

"We were talking about a *book*. Do you have to eaves-drop on everything like a goddam wiretapper?"

"Couldn't help it, man. What am I supposed to do, put cotton in my ears?"

"Put your earphones on and listen to the Stones."

"Thought I'd pick up a little education for a change," Tommy said. "Did I hear you say some girl in a story waited seven years for a dude while he was in jail?"

"Yeah. What about it?"

"Who'd wait seven years?"

"Sonia, the character in the book," Gary said. "And me. I would."

"You'd wait seven years for a chick?"

"For the right one, yeah."

"*Right one*. Man, what else you been reading in that English class, *Bride Magazine?*"

"Go to hell, Tommy. I got a girl I like. You met Diane."

"Yeah, she's something else."

"So. That's why I'd wait, if she was sick or something. Like I hope she'll wait for me."

"Wait—*wait?* You *think* too much. Wait for what?"

"Til I can get around."

Tommy yawned. "So how long you figure that'll be for you, couple more months?"

Gary hesitated. "Longer, probably."

"How come?"

"Kimball says—Kimball says he doesn't think I'm ever going to walk."

The room was quiet except for the wall speaker. "*Calling Dr. Rhodes. Calling Dr. Rhodes.*"

Tommy cleared his throat. "Did I hear you right, man?"

"Yeah."

"When did he tell you?"

"This morning."

"Whooo, boy. Well, you know doctors talk shit, don't you? I wouldn't give a counterfeit two bucks for what doctors told me. Constantine, my doctor, says I'm gonna go to my grave in leg braces. I told him to go to hell. They always hand you that gloomy stuff, so that when you're walking you'll say, 'Oh, Dr. So-and-so, you're such a god! What a miracle!' " Tommy paused. "You don't believe what he told you, do you?"

"No."

"Good," Tommy said. "Good. Jesus, how did your old lady take it?"

"She knew. Kimball told her before."

"And she's been chirping around like that, knowing? My old lady heard the word brace and she collapsed. What about your dad?"

"He's cool, too. Nobody whines at my house."

"And Diane? Did you tell her yet?"

"No."

"Going to?"

"Oh, well, sure. I have to—I guess."

"Yeah, may as well. That way you'll find out."

"Find out?"

"Sure, find out. If she's an angel she'll stick with you— for a while at least. And if she's not, she'll take off."

Gary was silent.

"Don't worry, buddy," Tommy said, "she'll probably hang in. She looks like one of those types that dig playing nurse. But even if she takes off, kid, don't sweat it. You'll find somebody else. A therapist, maybe. Very good-looking therapists at Phillips. When's she coming—Diane?"

"Tonight—after supper."

"So tell her. But be sure and tell her that what Kimball says is a crock. Tell her, *forget doctors*, you'll be walking out of Phillips in six months. Yaah—hooo!" Tommy started coughing.

Telling everybody else had been nothing, Gary thought. So how come with Diane . . . ?

"Whew—*ooh*, boy," Tommy said finally, taking a deep breath. "The *pain!* You know, maybe you're not so bad off feeling nothing down below? I swear to God."

"Christ, what a dumb thing to say."

"O.K., O.K., you're right," Tommy said. "I was just—that was just a way of talking. I know it's no joke when you can't feel." He paused. "I knew this guy once at Mt. Olive Hospital, had no feeling in his legs. He was sitting near a radiator one day in his chair. Just sittin' there, a bunch of us. And all of a sudden there was this raunchy smell. His flesh was—"

"God, Tommy, will you cut the gory stories!"

"O.K., man, O.K., I apologize. I know you don't like hearing that stuff, but I'm telling you for your own good—because I like you. You take everything *too personal*, you know?"

"Forget the advice!" Gary shouted. "First of all, I don't believe half the crap you tell me, and even if it was true, who wants to listen to that depressing garbage? A little positive thinking, man," he said, forcing himself to calm down. The tongs seemed to be jabbing him like two screwdrivers puncturing a coconut. "I mean, I don't believe in Santa Claus. I know there's some gross stuff in the world, but must you go *looking* for it? Jesus, you know what you ought to try out for—reporter for the *National Enquirer*—if you knew how to write the goddam alphabet."

"Don't snap, buddy," Tommy said. "You think I *like* blood and guts? Well, I don't. Blood and guts are just *around*. You'll find out. Life's tough."

"You're telling me?" Gary's head was hurting now. A moist film blurred his vision. "Your doctor says you'll probably be back trimming pussy willows next spring," he said. "My doctor says I'll probably never walk, and you're telling me life is tough?" Gary closed his eyes. *Cool it.* Where was his mother, anyway? If she were here, Tommy would shut up.

"Listen, Gary," Tommy said, "I don't want to mess up your pretty pictures, I don't. You're younger than me, and—"

"Big deal," Gary interrupted. "One crummy year younger, Frechette. My birthday's a week from Saturday."

"So, a year's a year," Tommy said. "You're younger than me, and even if you been this big football player, you still been a protected schoolboy. Here's my point. Life's tough, buddy, so *you* gotta be tough."

Gary listened. The phlegm and the hardness had gone out of Tommy's voice now. He was sounding like Buck giving a half-time talk. Or like Kimball. In the mirror Gary watched Tommy rising up slowly on his elbow again.

"You were tough with your body, man, probably will be again," Tommy went on. "But you gotta be tough in the head, too, kid. Don't take everything to heart, or you'll end up in looneyville or—down the drain."

"What do you mean, down the drain?" Gary asked.

"I ain't saying. That'd get me into another story. Just take it to mean wiping yourself out. That's what some guys do, when they take things too much to heart. I've known a few, but my lips are cemented shut, man."

"I'd never do that," Gary said.

"That's cool. Just start getting tough in the head, so you keep on thinking like that. No matter how many chicks take off on you, you gotta stay cool. Other fish in the sea, man. And don't pay attention to stories. Stories are for passing the time. Just *words.*"

Tommy was right—he had to get tough. Stop letting the stories get to him. Tell Diane tonight.

"Hey," Tommy said, "here comes somebody—your old lady?"

"Ma?"

"No, it's me, Gary. Hi!"

"Diane? I thought—"

Diane rushed in and leaned over the frame. "I just came by for a second, Gary," she said, out of breath. "They called me to come into work tonight, but I told them I could only make it if I stopped by the hospital first. I've got to go soon. Your mother's not here?"

"She went downstairs for something. Diane—I—"

"Good, I hope she stays for awhile." Diane bent over and kissed him on the lips. "How are you?" she whispered. "Hi," she said to Tommy.

"Hi." Tommy coughed.

"I'm—O.K.," Gary said. Man, a shock, seeing Diane all of a sudden in her brown-and-white-check bakeshop uniform—smelling clean like lemon soap. Don't go to work, Diane, he felt like saying. Got something to tell you. *May as well find out.* "So—how's everything with you?" he asked.

Diane sighed. "Oh, all right. I'm sick of work, though. Wish I didn't have to go. But if I make enough, I could buy a used car, maybe, so I can come out and see you at Phillips. By the way, Billy says hi. He was telling me today about the things you and him used to do in grade school—putting fake dog do on the teacher's desk—"

"Not me." Gary smiled. "*He* did that."

"Well, you two must've been some characters. Anyway, did you find out any more about when you're going?"

"Yeah," he said slowly. "Kimball told me today."

"How much longer?"

"Until I go to Phillips? Uh, about another month." Gary breathed heavily. Tommy was coughing his head off. Maybe he should ask Diane to pull the curtains. *If she's an angel, she'll stick . . .*

"Let's see." Diane sat down on the stool. "Four more weeks. If I keep clearing forty a week, that's one hundred sixty, and I've already got about three hundred twenty in the bank. Can I get a car for that, do you think, Gary? What is that, four hundred eighty?"

"Yeah, four eighty," Gary said. "I don't know." *Tell her now.* Get it over with. She'll probably hang in. Type that digs playing nurse.

"Can't get nothing but a piece of junk for four eighty."

Diane turned to Tommy. "No?"

Jesus, Gary thought, Tommy the wiretapper at it again. Screw Tommy. *Pull the curtain, Diane.*

"Only thing you could get'd be like a Ford Galaxie, maybe, late sixties," Tommy went on, "or an Impala coupe, same age. Nothing newer."

"Gary, what do you think," Diane was asking. "Should I buy a car?"

"I don't know. Come closer, Diane," he whispered, "I want to—let's talk privately."

"Sure, Gary. I'll talk to you later, Tommy," she called. She pulled the stool closer to the frame. "What is it? Want me to pull the curtain?"

"No—no, my mother'll be coming. Just lean over, Diane. Hey, we're alone."

She smiled. "Practically the first time. I miss you so much, Gary. The kids at school do, too. Mr. Ackerman's always giving reports about you over the P.A. Bobby Savino's heading up a carwash to raise money for you. And Ms. Treer's been so nice to me. I'm always talking to her about you. Was she here today?"

"Yeah."

"I looked for her after school. Did she give you work to dictate?"

"Yeah."

"We'll do it tomorrow, O.K.? 'Cause I have to go in a second. Wish I didn't, but they get so mad when I'm late. I miss you, Gary. I can't wait until you come back to school. It's no fun between classes anymore. No fun *in* classes either, but that's nothing new. I miss you coming over to my house—even my mother said the other day, 'Sure is quiet around here.' Remember last summer? My house after we came back from the shore? We'll do that again real soon, Gary. Next time—maybe it'll end different."

Gary blinked. She was putting her hand on his arm now. He could feel it.

"Did you get any more movement today?" she asked.

"A little."

"Good. You're working so hard. It won't be long now, I bet. I've got to go, Gary. Did the doctor say anything else?"

Gary closed his eyes. He could hear Tommy coughing quietly. "No— he said I'm doing pretty good."

She nodded. "Your right arm's one hundred percent better, isn't it? Did he say anything about your left arm?"

"No."

"I can't stand leaving, Gary. But I don't want to be late

again. They're so mean when I'm late. Anything else, Gary?" she whispered. "Anything else private?"

"I'm glad you came. I didn't expect it—I wish— Diane?"

"Yes?"

"Diane—my mother's inviting the coaches and tutors up on my birthday, a week from Saturday, after the game. You come, O.K.?"

"Sure. I already got your present. I hope you'll be able to use it real soon." Diane got up. " 'Bye, Gary." She kissed him again. "I hate leaving." She let go of the edge of the frame reluctantly. "See you tomorrow . . ." she said as she turned away. "'Bye."

"Diane?" She was gone. He closed his eyes. Why hadn't he told her? What the hell had come over him? He'd always thought of himself as tough—a guy with a strong character. So how come, now, in the crunch, he had acted like a goddam coward?

chapter **11**

Football builds character. Ann sat in the first row of bleachers watching Buck pace back and forth at the 50-yard line, hands in his pockets, a soft, floppy hat on his head. Buck would swear that manhood was being earned and lost on that field right now. Gary believed it. Just yesterday she had read in his journal: "Football has taught me all I know about quick thinking, courage, sportsmanship, and cooperation."

"New Bridge 7, Winstead 7, in this Saturday, October 23 Homecoming game," the nasal voice over the P.A. announced. *"Winstead's ball on the 35 now. Second and nine. Haskins, number 12, carrying. No gain on the play. Time out, Winstead Warriors."*

Ann pulled up her coat collar. A damp chill was in the air. All around her, spectators crushed together under plaid blankets. Band members on her left stomped their feet and blew on chafed fingers. Cheerleaders with bare thighs jumped and jiggled for warmth. Ann looked at the scoreboard clock that was stopped at six minutes to go in the last quarter and wished she could push it ahead. Six minutes of playing time would expand into at least another quarter hour of shivering in the stands. She had only come to the game on account of Mrs. Madden's invitation for afterward. They weren't calling it a party. Just a few friends —teachers and kids—stopping up at the hospital for a piece of cake in honor of Gary's eighteenth birthday.

Ann heard the whistle, watched Buck and Wally exhort the team, saw Jason—barely visible under his blue helmet— gargle a mouthful of water and spit it on the ground. A cry went up in the stands. She wished she could get into the spirit of things, merge with the crowd, but her heart wasn't in it.

"We've got the pep, we've got the steam . . ." the cheerleaders chanted shrilly, waving blue and white pompoms. The crowd swayed. Down the row at the 30-yard line Ann thought she saw Diane in a tall, visored hat and blue uniform. Diane had been on her mind all week. She must know by now what the doctor had told Gary.

The P.A. crackled. *"Second and nine, Winstead's ball. Haskins fading back . . ."*

Hoarse cries echoed across the field. The defense swarmed, and a cheer went up.

"Quarterback Alan Haskins, number 12, sacked on the play."

Sacked, drubbed, clobbered, Ann thought—the vocabulary of a sport that was always able to spew forth one more violent word or image to describe itself. What would Buck and Gary say now—that Haskins was developing character out there under that pileup? Ann watched the bodies peel away until Haskins sprang to his feet. A better man? Did sacking, clobbering, make you tougher? Did suffering make you strong?

"A loss of five yards. Third and fourteen on the 30. Haskins handing off to Grissolm . . ."

"Hit 'im!" yelled the man next to Ann, as Grissolm, charging out of bounds, knocked a yard marker out of the linesman's hands that careened toward the bench. Ann ducked. In the old days she'd gone with pleasure to her high school and college games. She'd lent support at the sidelines to Mike when he played touch football and had watched the Superbowl with him. Lately the faintest possibility of bodies colliding jarred her.

"A penalty on the play—against New Bridge. Putnam, number 51, unnecessary roughness, 15 yards. First down, Winstead on the 45 . . ."

Ann watched Buck pull out Putnam, number 51, as the visiting team booed. Buck slung his arm around Putnam's shoulders. Unnecessary roughness. Well, wasn't it better, at least, that Putnam was working out his aggression here instead of on a street corner? Still, the crack of helmet on helmet and the wrenching of bodies as Winstead eked out an extra yard. . . . Either there was something wrong with the game or with her, Ann thought.

Whichever it was, she didn't have to stick it out until the end. Nobody would care if she stayed or left. She could wait in the car until the game was over and then go to the hospital. She stood up, moved quickly so she wouldn't block anyone's view.

"Haskins carrying for Winstead . . ."

105

Walking away from the center of the crowd along the track that encircled the field, Ann turned to take a last look at the scoreboard. The game would probably finish in a 7–7 tie. A good way to end, she thought, nobody a loser. Buck wouldn't see it that way, though. Mike, she remembered, had always said that ending in a tie was like kissing your sister. As she reached a section of empty bleachers, Ann heard the crunch of flying cinders. She turned around.

"Ms. Treer! Ms. Treer!" Diane called. "I've been looking for you! I heard you were here." Her cheeks were ruddy; wisps of blond hair escaped from her hat.

"Hi!" Ann waited for her.

"Some kids told me they saw you," Diane said. "I've been looking all over. Whew! You aren't leaving, are you?"

"I—"

She breathed quickly. "Aren't you going up to see Gary? He told me you were."

"Yes, I'm going."

"Good." Diane hobbled toward the bleachers in her high white boots. "Can we sit down a second?" she asked, pointing to her feet.

"Sure." A gust of wind whipped the two of them. Ann pulled her coat around her and sat down. Beyond them in the stands the crowd roared. Diane jumped up.

"*A fumble on the play! Recovered by . . . Lovett, New Bridge. Lovett carrying . . . returns the ball to the Winstead . . . 40-yard line! First and ten, New Bridge.*"

"It's our ball, Ms. Treer! Jason's doing good. Maybe they can win it yet." Diane, gathering her uniform skirt close, sat down again. "Gary would be so happy if we won. We haven't beat Winstead in four years." Taking off a boot and curling one stockinged foot underneath her, she turned to Ann. "I should be watching the game but, I don't know, since Gary's not playing, I can't concentrate. This is a terrible place to talk, isn't it? Is it all right, Ms. Treer? My catching you like this? Were you going somewhere?"

"It's all right. I was getting a little chilly. What's on your mind?"

"I came looking for you a couple of times after school, but you weren't in your room."

"I'm sorry I missed you. I've been wondering how you were."

"The reason I came was—because Gary told me something last Sunday, and I've been thinking about it the whole week. . . ."

Ann watched her. "Yes?"

Diane twisted her necklace. "He says the doctor thinks he might never walk, Ms. Treer."

"I know," Ann said.

"He told you the day he found out, didn't he?"

"Mr. Lausch and the doctor did—before."

"Gary knew for two days before he told me," she said. "I think he wanted to spare me, Ms. Treer, but I told him he shouldn't have felt that way. He should've told me right away. I've been thinking. . . ."

Band music and a crescendo of cheers from the stands drowned out Diane's words. *"Berger's pass to Lovett was complete. New Bridge's ball on the 34. First and ten. New Bridge time out."*

The band music faded and Diane moved nearer to Ann. "I've been thinking, Ms. Treer, ever since Gary told me," Diane said, lowering her voice. "And I've got this idea. I haven't told anyone about it yet—not even Gary. I want to ask you what you think first."

Ann buried her chin in her coat. Diane had taken off her marching hat now, and her hair blew in the wind. "What is it?" Ann asked.

"*New Bridge's ball on the 34. Three and a half minutes of play left in the game.*"

"First of all," Diane said, "I told Gary that I'll wait for him no matter how long it takes, and if he can't walk, well then, that's all right, too. . . ."

"That must have meant a lot to him."

Diane smiled. "Sometimes he acts like he's big and tough, but when I said that, he—well, he wouldn't want me to tell, so I won't. Anyway, Ms. Treer, this is my idea. See what you think."

"*Pass complete to Lovett on the Winstead 21! A gain of thirteen yards on the play.*" Spectators stomped their feet on the bleachers.

Diane held her hair back with one hand to keep it from blowing. "I'm thinking of not going to college next year."

Ann tuned out the P.A. and the noise of the crowd. "Why not?" she asked.

"So I can take care of Gary."

"Will that be necessary?"

"You mean his mother could do it, right?"

"Well, yes."

"But if I took care of Gary, she could go back to her job." Ann said nothing.

"You don't think it's a good idea, do you?" Diane asked.

"I think it sounds very generous. Gary'll need lots of help and moral support next year, but I'm not sure you'd be doing the most for him by giving up your own schooling."

"Isn't it good to give up something for somebody you love?"

"Not if you both lose out by it."

"Who'll be losing out? I don't care that much about going to college anyway."

"Everybody doesn't have to. Just be sure that if you *do*, it's for the right reasons, and if you *don't*, it's for the right reasons."

"My reason will be I love Gary and want to be with him."

"I don't know how that rates as a reason not to go to school," Ann said, "but if you want to be with him, you'd better consider going to college, because that's most likely where he'll be."

"How could he, if he can't walk? *He* says he's going to walk, but the doctor says not."

"Who says a person has to walk to go to college? Do you think with your feet?"

"So he could go—in a wheelchair?"

"Sure, that's what Dr. Kimball says."

"Next year? Like everybody else?"

"I guess time will tell about that."

"Oh. Well, Gary and I are going to have to talk about all this." Diane let go of her hair so that it swirled around her head again. "If Gary can go to college next year, that'll make him really happy, because he's always wanted to. Me, I don't care that much. So what do you think, then, Ms. Treer? Think I should go to the same school as Gary?"

"What's the rush?" Ann asked. "You have plenty of time to decide, don't you?"

"Not really. I have to put in applications now."

"Shouldn't you talk to your parents?"

"I guess so. To tell you the truth, my mother's not going to like it if I go to a certain school because of Gary. She's already saying things like 'Don't get tied down.' But you know, I just made up my mind. I'm going to the same school as Gary. That way I can help him. I'll tell him today. He'll really be glad. Thanks, Ms. Treer, for talking to me."

"Sure. But you don't have to decide today, Diane."

"Break that tie! Break that tie!"

"Look, Ms. Treer!" Diane grabbed her arm.

"Nine yards and goal to go for the New Bridge Lions; fifty-eight seconds remaining in the game."

The action was in front of them now. Back at the 50-yard line, cheerleaders somersaulted. Buck, mopping his brow, paced. A wave of spectators drifted out of the stands and hugged the sidelines near the goal. Ann wandered, along with Diane, onto the grass at the 10-yard line.

"Berger, number 10, sweeps to the left. Tackle made by Mahoney, number 14. A gain of two yards on the play, Second and goal to go for the New Bridge Lions here at Scott Memorial Field, with 31 seconds left in the game!"

"We want a touchdown, we want a touchdown!"

Ann felt the crush of bodies behind her as fans circled in. Diane, hanging onto Ann's arm, bobbed up and down.

"Break that tie! Break that tie!"

"Berger fading back for a pass . . . looking for a receiver . . ."

Ann watched 88—Jason—limber as an aerialist, sidestep an opponent in the end zone and leap into the air. *Some dude catching a pass isn't what football's about,* she remembered his saying to her. Too bad it wasn't, she thought, as Jason lunged for the ball and pulled it to him with grace and precision.

"Pass complete, received by Lovett. New Bridge 13, Winstead 7! Seven seconds remaining in the game, six, five, four . . ."

Ann heard her own voice merging with the general swell

of sound, felt the rough twill of the uniform as she returned Diane's hug.

"We did it! We did it!" Diane shouted. "It's so much better than a tie!"

chapter **12**

"Happy birthday, dear Gary, happy birthday to you . . ."
"Thanks. Thanks, everybody." Not exactly what he'd
ever pictured as an eighteenth-birthday celebration, but not
too bad as the official start of his new life. The tongs, of
course, made celebrating a pretty ridiculous word, but another week and he'd be out of them. The cotton wadding
on his feet to protect the skin break on his heel wasn't
making him too happy. Still, that was temporary. His arms
were definitely gaining. And, what the hell—a party was
the people at it, and everybody important was here. Diane,
right by him, practically touching his shoulder. His parents
fussing around with the cake. Jason, Buck, Wally, and

Treer reflected in the mirror. Tommy, out of the room now, had woken him up at seven in the morning coughing and singing "Happy Birthday" through his nose. Billy would be coming up later, and Dottie and Dr. Kimball had stopped in early. Oh, yeah. Mr. Ackerman from school and Pastor Shafer had been in, too. Not a bad day. Lots of cards from kids. A tape recorder as a gift from the team. An electric razor from Diane. A Stones tape from Tommy. Other books and tapes from friends. His mother, he saw in the mirror, was wetting her fingers now and quickly putting out the single candle on the cake, as if that was the ordinary thing with birthday candles. Always looking for ways to smooth things over.

"That's a beautiful cake, Mrs. Madden," Treer said.

"Isn't it? The women at the church made it." His mother tilted it for Gary to see better in the mirror. "The nurses suggested I take it down the hall to the pantry to slice it. Dad's gone down. I'll be back in a few minutes, Gary."

"O.K.," he said. "We'll play party games while you're gone." His mother, on her way out, gave him one of those hurt looks, like she always did now, when he made a joke about himself. Gotta laugh, Ma! "Jason, old buddy," he said, "what game you want to play?"

"Uh—pin the tail on Coach Hammer?"

"I heard that, *boy*." Wally grinned. "You watch your step, or I'll come after you some dark night with a sheet over my head."

Buck chuckled awkwardly. Treer had on her snobby look. Race jokes weren't her thing.

"Hey, Gary." Jason moved in next to Diane. "Did Coach Hammer tell you what happened between him and Crowell, the math teacher?"

"No," Gary said.

Wally edged closer. "What?"

Jason cleared his throat. "See, Crowell claimed he was going to flunk Putnam in math and make him ineligible. So Coach Hammer goes to Crowell and asks him not to—"

"You—where'd you get that?" Wally asked.

"Take it easy now and let me tell the rest of it," Jason said. "The coach goes, 'Putnam's one of my boys!' So Crowell agrees, 'Just for you, Coach, I'll give the kid another chance. O.K., Putnam, want to pass math? What's seven plus six?' Putnam takes a wild guess. 'Twelve?' he says. Crowell groans. 'Hopeless case, Coach. He flunks.' 'Aw, come on,' Coach Hammer begs Crowell, 'let the poor kid have one more go at it. He only missed by *two!*' "

Everybody was laughing.

"Crowell's my tutor," Gary said, "He might be stopping up here today. I'll check with him if it's true."

Even Treer was laughing. So was Wally. Was he really dumb like they made him out to be? Dumb, maybe, about what to say to people different from him. The other Wally Hammer jokes had to do with what a stud he was. Could you tell that about a guy just by the way he looked and talked? Could you tell if a girl was sexy for that matter? Diane looked sexy, but she behaved like a nun. Well, not a nun exactly. Anyway, get a load of Wally now with his big shoulders and smooth chin, leaning close to Treer. Giving her the eye. Looking her up and down. She was ignoring him. Good for her.

Jason and the coaches were rapping about the game. Oh, terrific—Diane had put her hand on his arm, was massaging his biceps like the nurses did. He looked up at her. Too bad she'd only touch him when his parents weren't around. Well, after all, he'd been that way himself. He'd never even held Diane's hand when her mother was in the room.

Diane lowered her head now so that it touched his shoulder. "I have something to tell you later," she whispered. "I'll stay after everybody goes."

"Yeah? What? What is it?"

"Tell you later."

She squeezed his arm. He sure felt better since he'd worked up the nerve to tell her the whole truth. Why had he been so scared to? Her reaction had been beautiful. *If she's an angel, she'll stick.* She was an angel, she was going to stick—but there was one thing that bothered him. Was he being selfish letting her? Nobody loved going places more than she did. Almost all their best times had centered on action—sports events, dances, walking in the park, skiing. If she stuck with him, she'd be giving up all that. Hell, ridiculous! He wasn't forcing her to do anything. What was he supposed to do, send her away for her own good?

"Hey, Billy!"

"Here comes the cake!"

Gary felt Diane let go of his arm. He heard the rattle of a cart, a flurry of confusion, his mother's voice.

"We have enough cake for an army," she said. "Dad's taking some to the nurses. Bill Berger's here, Gary."

Billy, standing behind Diane, waved. "Hi, Gary."

"Hi." Billy, All-American jock. Bruised cheek, blond hair still damp from the showers. Where you been this week, Billy? he felt like asking, but Billy was talking to Wally Hammer.

"Hey, Bill," Gary called, "congratulations! After four years you finally whupped 'em, heh?"

"Yeah," Billy said shyly. "Some game. A real cliff-hanger. We—I wish you'd been there." Billy fumbled with the paper plate that was offered him. "Can I help pass these around, Mrs. Madden?"

"No, no. Just enjoy yourself. Talk to Gary. Everything's taken care of."

Talk to Gary, his mother had said, but Billy was turning to Wally again. Hey, buddy, nothing to say to me? Me, the guy you roomed with at football camp? The guy who always saved you a place in the lunch line? The guy who used to help you put snow down your sister's back in grade school?

"Gary, shall I set aside your cake until you're on your stomach?"

"Let me have it now, Ma, with everybody else. I promise I won't choke." Sad smile from her again. Why did everything he said make her sad? He wasn't doing it on purpose.

"All this activity, Gary—let's wait—I'm involved with the guests—"

"Diane'll feed me."

"Sure," Diane said. "Here . . ." she reached for his plate.

His mother held onto it, handed her another one. "Here's yours, Diane." She paused. "Gary, if you really want your cake now, I'll give it to you." She broke off a bite-size piece and held it to his lips. "Chew carefully. We don't want to—"

"Diane can give it to me, Ma," he said.

Diane held her own plate uncertainly.

"I know, I know she can," his mother said. "It makes no difference. I'll do it. Let Diane eat hers. Don't you want her to enjoy her cake?"

He glanced at Diane, opened his mouth, and nibbled at the bit his mother offered. Diane slowly lifted her plastic fork to her mouth.

Wally came up behind Mrs. Madden. "Terrific cake," he said.

"As good as my wife's," Buck called. "And while you're all quiet because your mouths are full, let me say something." He raised his cake plate in the air and waited for everyone's attention. The room was quiet. "Here's to Gary," he said. "Nothing can beat this kid, nothing." He looked from one of them to another. "I've had a lot of boys play for me, and he's—well, I never say any *one* of them's the greatest, but he's—he's right up there at the top. And this is a fine party. And I plan to be here at many more parties for Gary Madden."

"I second that," Ms. Treer said. "And that's got to be the shortest speech Coach Lausch ever made."

"Yeah," Gary said, "but he left out my favorite part about beating their asses in." They were all laughing except his mother. Just said ass, Ma. Part of the anatomy.

"Well, a lot of things go in my locker-room speech, Gary," Buck blushed. "But I try to spare the women that kind of talk."

"You mean you have a double standard?" Ms. Treer asked.

"Yes," Buck said. "I believe there's a certain way to act on the field and another way to act in mixed company."

Mrs. Madden nodded. "I agree."

"Coach Hammer always acts the same," Jason said. "Can't take him anywhere."

Buck ignored the smiles. "Some of my boys think I'm old-fashioned, I know that, but I believe men are one way, and women are another, and the difference was meant to be."

Gary scanned the faces. Billy and Jason looked bored. His mother was agreeing. Diane, listening politely. Treer—ha. Treer was biting her lip as if she either wanted to keep herself from laughing or from arguing with Buck. What the heck, Treer, argue, just for the fun of it.

"Out on the field," Buck went on, "that's the place to be a man. That's the place to give lumps and take 'em without hollering, to curse if you want to, to make your jokes about women, if you're that kind of a fellow. But off the field," Buck looked at Mrs. Madden, "that's the place to be a gentleman, to watch your language, to show courtesy toward women, even though some of 'em'd rather you didn't."

"You talk like men are nasty, Coach," Jason said. "We're not all that bad."

"We don't want to be," Buck told him, "but it's in the nature. I have the highest respect for women. They help us pull ourselves up."

Treer was finally going to put a word in.

"Do you have to give and take lumps to be a man?" she asked.

"Well," Buck said, "maybe it's not right, and I'm not saying I like it this way, but we sure measure a man by his physical size and strength. The little fellow isn't usually respected, or the fellow who avoids a contest."

"Let's face it," Wally said. "Appearance counts, on the field and off."

"Yes, I like to see a man *look* masculine," Mrs. Madden said. "Some of these boys with the long hair and feminine clothes . . ."

"Don't worry, Ma, we won't let any of those freaks in here," Gary said. He yawned. Man, when would they leave? He was glad they came, but he was getting tired, anxious to hear what Diane had to say to him.

"I have to be going," Treer was saying.

Must've read his mind. Everybody was making good-bye

noises. Excellent cake. Thanks for coming. Well, the party was over. Eighteen years old. How about that. He was legal. A man. He glanced up at Diane. "You're going to stay?" he whispered.

She nodded.

"Happy birthday, Gary," Treer said, putting an envelope on the bedside table. "That's a card," she said. "A Tea Runner original. See you Monday."

"Thanks, Ms. Treer. We'll discuss the play, right?"

"Right."

Treer put her hand on the frame. "Good-bye," she said with a smile, as if there were a secret between them.

They were all gathered around the bed, looking down at him now. "So long, Billy, Coach Lausch . . ." he said. Something funny about Billy's expression. What's wrong, old buddy?

"Take it easy, Gary," Billy said. He turned away quickly.

" 'Bye, Coach Hammer, Ms. Treer . . ." Wally was staring at him, his eyes traveling up and down. Did he do that to everybody?

"Mrs. Madden . . ." Buck said. He was leaning over the frame to whisper to her.

His mother put her hand to her face. Then a silence, with everybody's eyes on him. A couple of whispers, a rush of farewells. His mother pressing the button for the nurse. What the hell was up? He felt O.K. Had somebody spotted another skin break? "Hey," he said. "What's happening? Something wrong?" He looked in the mirror, but he could only see the edge of the sheet and the reflections of Buck, Wally, and Treer on their way to the door. His mother was handing Diane her coat.

"Hey, Ma? Diane's not leaving yet."

His mother came to him. "It's better if she does," she

whispered. "You've had an accident. Nothing serious. It'll be all right. I'm just going to say good-bye to everyone, and we'll take care of it."

"Accident? What?" He focused on the mirror again, but he couldn't see much.

"You're wet," Diane said quietly.

"Loose connection, man," Jason nodded. "We don't mind if you don't."

"*I mind!* Am I wet . . . all over? Ma?"

"The sheet's wet, Gary. I'm going to find Sister Marie. I think everyone should go now."

"I'm going to split, Gary," Jason said in his ear. "Your old lady wants us out. Be seeing you real soon."

"So long, Jay. Thanks for coming. Diane? Hey, Diane? Can you stay in the lounge until—"

"Sure. Just let me tell Billy. He's going to wait downstairs and give me a ride home."

"You mean, you'll be holding him up if you stay?"

"He won't mind. I'll tell him."

"No, forget it. Take the ride."

"It's O.K., Gary. I'll walk home."

"No, go ahead. Let me get dry."

"Please, Gary, I *want* to stay."

"I want you to go." His mother was back by the bed, helping Diane on with her coat.

"I'll come tomorrow, Gary."

"Yeah," he said.

Diane touched his arm, spoke low enough so his mother couldn't hear. "It's nothing," she said. "Your accident's nothing. Nobody minds. Don't be upset. I'll see you tomorrow. I want to talk to you about next year. About me going to whatever college you go to next year, so I can help you. I love you, Gary."

"Yeah," he said.

Yeah? Was that all? It'd be so easy to say *I love you, too.* Why didn't he? What an ass he was! Some eighteen-year-old *man.* You can tell a man by the look of him, Wally had just said. Well, this was the look of Gary Madden: flat on his back, feet padded, lying under a wet sheet and didn't even know it until somebody told him. Diane wanted to go to college with him next year. Because she loved him? No, because she wanted to play nurse!

"So long, Diane," he said. She gave him a look and turned to go. She had never been so beautiful. He deserved to lose her.

chapter **13**

"I'm going to raise you a couple of degrees higher than yesterday, O.K., Gary?" Dottie fixed the pillows under his head, knees, and feet, and strapped him to the tilt table next to his bed.

"O.K.," he said. Dizzy-making, this contraption that was gradually supposed to be getting him used to being vertical after six weeks of lying flat. Not half as bad as getting turned on the Stryker, though. Oh, man, time was passing, over two weeks since his birthday. Things were looking up —for real, looking up. No more frame. A regular bed now. *And no more tongs and weights.* Kimball had taken out the tongs on Monday, easy as anything. Freedom, almost—except for the stiff neck brace that was digging into his chin.

"I'll tilt you now and get you back into bed again before your English teacher comes," Dottie said. "Expecting anybody else this afternoon?"

"No," he said.

"Diane's not coming?"

"No."

Dottie was checking the straps, bustling around. "I haven't seen Diane for a couple of days," she said. "Is everything all right?"

"Yeah."

"Yeah?" She raised her eyebrows. "You sure? Your mother's coming back, isn't she? Where did she go today?"

"To the school to talk to Ackerman, the principal."

"How come?"

"To ask about my getting into college. I didn't want her to, but she went anyway. She's worried I won't be prepared. You know, this year's work."

"Are you worried?"

"Naa. I'm learning. In English, anyway. And history's not too bad. Mrs. Purdy keeps canceling out—that's what's bugging my mom. Math's a snap. Crowell thinks I've got brain damage, so he's taking it easy. Reviewing stuff I had in seventh grade."

"And you're not telling him different?" Dottie tilted the table.

"Why should I?" His feet pointed down now, and his head rose slowly.

"How is it with your head up, bubby, better than yesterday?"

"The room's starting to swim," he said. Dottie held his hand. He could feel where she touched him. Not the same sensation as before the accident—sort of like his hand was asleep but still alive somewhere deep down under layers of numbness and prickles. "Man, I'm seeing circles, gold circles." The walls were buckling and waving.

"Takes time, Gary." She patted his arm. "You're coming along so well. You can sit up in bed now, to eat. Your sore foot's all healed. Another couple of days and you'll be in a wheelchair. Less than two weeks and you'll be off to Phillips, with Tommy—feeding yourself, learning to dress yourself. How is it now?"

"I'm hearing voices."

"Anybody I know?"

"No . . . whispers, and sirens."

"That'll disappear a little bit every day. In a couple of weeks you'll be able to take this table straight up."

He closed his eyes, but that made the dizziness worse, so he opened them again. "Dottie, I'll be able to wheel my own chair, right?"

"Maybe not at first, but real soon."

"When I start college—say I'm still in a chair," he said. "I won't have to have anybody following me around, will I? I mean a nurse, or anything?"

"You should be able to do almost everything for yourself. Why?"

His ears were ringing. It was hard to concentrate. "Diane —Diane wants to come with me to college, wherever I go."

"Is that bad?"

"No, no, that's good. Just that she wants to comes so she can take care of me. That's what she says."

"And you don't want to be taken care of?"

He tried to ignore the whispering voices. "I want to take care of myself," he said.

"Good." Dottie adjusted the pillow under his head. "Nothing wrong with accepting a little help when you need it, though."

"But . . ." He pictured Diane pushing him in a chair, taking notes for him—like a mother taking a baby to college. "I want to be independent."

"Sure you do. You'll be able to do a lot of things for yourself—wheel your own chair, write—"

"When will I be able to write?"

"It won't be long now. I'll show you something later. A trick."

"To write?"

She nodded.

He caught her eye. "I—I lied to you before," he said.

"Lied? What about?"

"Everything's not O.K. with me and Diane."

She laid her hands on his face. "Gary, what's bothering you, sweetie? What is it? What's happening with Diane?"

"Well . . . first I told her to leave on my birthday. I was embarrassed that night—and mad."

"And then?"

"She came the next day and said all that stuff about taking care of me, and that made me mad again. So I said I wanted to think about it. And she must've thought I didn't want her to go to college with me. And she probably thought I wanted her to stay away, but I didn't mean that. I thought she'd come, but she hasn't. I can't write. I couldn't call when I was still in tongs."

"You could now. Want me to put a call through later?"

He hesitated. "I don't know."

"She's waiting for you to call, and you're waiting for her. Now isn't that dumb? Maybe she doesn't realize you can talk on the phone."

"Yeah, maybe." Plus the fact that he'd told her to leave. As usual, he was the clod who had clammed up when he ought to speak.

"I'll put a call through for you after your lesson," Dottie said.

"I'll think about it."

"For sure, hon. She'll be so happy. Hey, here comes your mother. Hi, Mrs. Madden. He says he feels like he's swimming. On the beach at Waikiki."

"Wouldn't that be nice." His mother laid her coat on the bed and came toward him with a large brown envelope. "I can't get over seeing him up like this," she said. "I have lots of news, Gary. I saw Mr. Ackerman."

"Excuse me, Mrs. Madden," Dottie said. "While you're here, I'm going to check on Mr. Ascher. I'll be back when it's time for you to come down, Gary."

"That's perfectly all right. You go ahead." Mrs. Madden smiled. "Listen to this, Gary. I have good news. Mr. Ackerman was very pleasant, very cooperative. He said he'll be over to see you again before you go to Phillips. Everybody at the high school sends you love—teachers, secretaries, everybody." She hugged the envelope to her. "They just couldn't stop talking about you. What a good athlete, a scholar. Mr. Ackerman agreed right away about Mrs. Purdy. She's canceled far too often. So—you'll like this—he asked Mrs. Treer if she could cover English *and* history, too, because she's certified in both, and I told him how you like to work with her. So he sent her a note, and she said yes, she'd do it. Isn't that good news?"

"Yeah, that's great."

"And then, guess what?"

"What?"

"The yearbook staff had to decide what to do with your position as sports editor, and they talked about it, and they took a vote, and guess what? They want you to be co-editor of sports. Isn't that wonderful?"

"What does it mean?"

"They want you to choose which pictures go in the book and to think of captions for them."

"What's the matter, couldn't they get anybody else?"

"Gary. It's a show of—faith in you."

"I guess so." That hurt look again. O.K., give her a break. "What're those?" He motioned to the envelope.

"Those are the pictures. This is the first batch for the sports section. Mr. Cole said I should bring them over right away, so you could get started. Look." She took them out of the envelope and held them up for him, one by one. "What are these, now?"

"Individuals of seniors on the football team."

"Oh, yes. There's Billy. That's good. Is there one of you?"

"Ought to be. They took 'em before the season started."

She shuffled through the pack. "Oh! Look . . ." She showed it to him.

Yeah, there he was. Crouched for action. Shoulders rocking forward, calves bulging. Jesus, he remembered that day —September 3. The heat. The one quart of Gatorade they had all had to share. Diane waiting for him in the stands after the photographer left. He looked at his mother, watched the change come over her face.

"It's a good picture, Gary. Dad'll enjoy that so much!"

A sob. She was trying to cover it up, but that's what it was. She was turning away from him. "Ma," he said.

"I'm sorry, Gary. . . ." She pressed her lips together. "It's been such a day, such a day. It's a wonderful picture."

"I don't look like that anymore, do I, Ma? That's why you did that, isn't it?"

"You look fine, Gary," she said. "You look almost like yourself now. Dr. Kimball says you'll start putting on weight. You'll fill out and build your muscles. I'll wash your hair tomorrow. He said I could. And you'll work at your studies. Mr. Ackerman will do all he can. And you'll do the best job as sports editor, I know you will." She breathed unevenly and spoke fast. "I have some other news, too. Dr. Kimball says I must let you—do more for yourself. He says I've done all I can for now. You'll be going to Phillips in a week or so, and they don't allow visitors there during the day. Dr. Kimball says I should go back to work as soon as possible."

"That's good, that's good, Ma. Don't worry. I'll be O.K."

"Are you sure?"

"Yeah, positive."

She fingered the edge of the envelope. "I wish I were," she said. "Sister Marie's excellent, but she's got so many other patients. The aides aren't used to shaving you. I worry about your meals."

"I'll eat, Ma. When are you going back?"

"The beginning of next week. Pastor Shafer's waited all this time without a replacement. He's got so much work piled up. He told me to say hello, by the way. He'll be in to see you too, before you go to Phillips."

"So you won't be here at all during the day?"

"No—no, I won't. I'll come just as early as I can in the evening, with Dad, like always. You'll do all right in the daytime, won't you? Oh, my!" The photographs slipped onto the floor. "Oh, look what I've done—what a mess!" She bent down to pick them up.

"Let me see mine again, Ma."

"I'll gather them up and put them away," she said, as if she hadn't heard him. "Look, the envelope's torn, I'll ask Sister Marie for another one." She stacked the photographs neatly. "I'll be right back."

"Ma, before you go out, tilt the big mirror this way, O.K.?"

"You look wonderful, Gary."

"Come on, Ma. Sister Marie said they're taking it away today. Let me see myself—come on."

Adjusting the mirror, she watched him. "A little more color in your cheeks, Gary, that's all. A few pounds and you'll look like your old self."

"Yeah. Go on, Ma, get the envelope. Go ahead."

"I'll be right back."

He waited to look in the mirror until she had gone. More of himself than he'd seen in six weeks. Jesus Christ. Was that his face? He stared. Were those his arms? Get a load of him—scars from the tongs still showed in the little bald patches on his head. His face—a ghost's; his hair, oily. He'd lost thirty-five pounds, Kimball had told him. He was *wasted*. Like something out of *Tales from the Crypt*. Look at his arms—atrophied, shrunken, so a girl about the size of Diane could get her hand all the way around them!

What were people thinking, telling him he looked wonderful? Did they think he was blind? Lies! Had he looked this bad on his birthday, when Diane was here? No wonder she'd stayed away. He'd been figuring on calling her tonight, like Dottie suggested. Until now. Until seeing himself the way he really was. How could they all stand looking at him, let alone faking it, telling him *soon you'll look like yourself*. The self they were talking about was that stranger in the football photograph with the big shoulders and muscular thighs. What a downer it must be for them to see him in the flesh. The Gary in the picture—*he* was the one they all remembered and expected to come back.

chapter 14

The door to Gary's room was open. Somebody was in there with him, Ann saw. It was Jason, cranking up the bed while he talked to him. Jason must have sneaked out of the pep rally at school just as she had. She stood in the hall for a minute watching Gary. Last week, just out of the tongs, he had looked gaunt and angular. She had told him he reminded her of an ascetic, a holy man. Now, sitting up in bed, his color was better, his hair had grown in. She knocked.

"Yeah, come on in."

"Beware of dog!" Jason called.

She entered.

Jason turned around. "I just want you to know, Ms. Treer, that when I tell Ackerman you're cutting the pep rally, he's not gonna like it one bit."

"Hi," Gary said.

"Hi." Ann took off her coat. "When I went to school, teachers ratted on students. What are *you* doing here?" she said to Jason.

"Saving my tail, is all. Somebody at that rally was setting off firecrackers. Ackerman was pissed!" he said to Gary. "Sorry, Ms. Treer—Ackerman was perturbed."

"You're early," Gary said.

"A little." She put down her books. "Mr. Crowell's coming when I finish. I promised I'd leave him some time."

Jason shook his head. "I'm ashamed of you, Ms. Treer, letting the school down, skipping the rally before the biggest game of the year."

"I'm there in spirit," she said. "What about you? Does Mr. Lausch know you left?"

"No way. He's too busy praying for a win." Jason paced back and forth by the bed. "You know what I'm praying for? That he don't have a heart attack over this game. Buck's never had a perfect season. He figures this may be his last chance before he retires."

"Buck's retiring?" Gary asked.

"He keeps threatening. If we win tomorrow, he'll quit while he's ahead, he says."

" 'Winning isn't everything,' " Gary said, " 'it's the only thing'—Vince Lombardi and Buck Lausch."

"Stupid quote," Jason said. "Lombardi got it laid on him by the press. I read where two other dudes said it before he did. Anyway, what he really said was 'Winning isn't everything, the *will* to win is the only thing.' "

"Yeah? Makes more sense," Gary said.

Ann sat down on the end of the bed. "Do you think Buck'll get his perfect season?"

Jason cracked his knuckles. "Gonna be tough. We got this mess lately where half the team thinks they're battling the other half. Seems like some of them yo-yo's want to lose."

"Who?"

"No names, buddy—some of them farm animals. You can guess who I mean."

"Who'd want to lose?"

Jason shrugged. "Not me."

"Some people, I guess," Ann said. "Winning's a strain. There's no place to go afterward except down."

"The heck with strain," Gary said. "I'd go for the win."

Jason nodded. "Hell, yeah. Well . . . I'd better be getting back for Buck's psych session. Just wanted to see your face, Gary. What do you say, give me five for luck tomorrow?"

"Sure, with a little help."

Jason, supporting Gary's arm, went through the motions of the handshake.

"Good luck, Jay."

"That's what counts," Jason said. He threw his jacket over his shoulder and headed for the door. "Have a good lesson. See you after the game tomorrow, Gary. 'Bye, Ms. Treer. I'll tell Ackerman to take it easy on you this time. Just don't cut any more pep rallies. Is that understood?"

"Perfectly. Good luck from me, too, Jason. Tell Buck the same."

They watched him go.

"So—how are you?" she asked when they were alone.

He shrugged.

"Multiple choice—super, pretty good, so-so, or down. Which?"

"So-so, I guess."

"Well, that's all right. That'll give you something to work up to. You're looking better than so-so."

"Still holy?"

"Less holy. Definitely down-to-earth. Why are you feeling so-so?"

"I don't know, . . . everything's the same all the time. I thought I was going to be glad to see my mother go back to work, but to tell you the truth, when she was here I wasn't as bored. She should've waited til I went to Phillips."

"You're going next week, right?"

"Yeah. I got a letter from Tommy, from Phillips. He makes the place sound so weird. Want to see it?"

"Sure."

"It's in the drawer there."

She took out the letter and opened it.

"Go on, read it. The spelling'll probably give you a heart attack."

"Don't worry, I'm used to that. I'll read it right. 'Hey, buddy, well here I am at good old P.I. This place is as much fun as poison ivy. Just kidding. It's not bad if you're hard up. The PTs (female) are good-looking, but not as stacked as Dottie. Naturally, my luck, I got a male PT, a black dude name of Ben Robie. Here they make you get up early, no loafing like at St. A's. I'm working my ass off and getting fit for leg braces. Some good people here— everybody but doctors called by first name. I got two room-mates, José, a Spanish guy who's a Jesus freak, and Howie, who's so spastic everybody's always kidding him saying, "Hey, Howie, what's up?" But he's a good guy. When are you coming? The food reeks. It's better at night here than

St. A's, because we play poker. I could tell you some good ones about the people here, but I won't. A couple of nice chicks, but some stuck-up ones, too. But you've got your woman, so you're not looking. See you soon. Your friend, Tom Frechette.' "

Ann folded the letter. "Sounds just like him."

"Yeah."

"How do you feel about going to Phillips?"

"I think I'm going to be by myself a lot."

"Why?"

"Visitors can only come out evenings. Jason's got no car. Billy—that kid's so damn busy, always visiting colleges. Diane . . ." He closed his eyes.

Ann paused. "You'll have company around the clock at Phillips."

He opened his eyes. "Yeah, but—the people—Jesus freaks and all that."

"That's Tommy's version. You'll have your own. I'm anxious to hear about it. Firsthand, from you."

"You're coming out, right—to tutor?"

"Oh, sure. Twice a week starting next Friday. You know what I'd like to do for an assignment? Make a tape of your impressions from the time you leave St. Agnes through the first couple of days at Phillips. Maybe your mother could bring it to me before I come out for the first time. O.K.?"

"O.K. What should I put on it?"

"Whatever you want. What the place looks like, who else is there, what you're doing. . . ."

"Yeah. 'Hi, there, Ms. Treer, just won two dollars off Howie the spastic!' Like that?"

"If that's the most interesting thing, go ahead. I've gotten a kick out of your journal. I miss it when I don't get a new installment. This week, for instance." She paused. "Diane hasn't been here at all, has she?"

"No."

"She wants to come. She told me."

"What did she say?"

"That she thinks you don't want to see her, and she doesn't understand why, because she was only trying to help you."

"I do want to see her."

"Then maybe you should tell her so."

"I'd call, but the phone's not . . . good."

"I'll give her a message if you want me to."

"Tell her I'd like to see her."

"She'll be relieved to hear that."

"When will you tell her?"

"I'll call her when I get home. How about if we start our session now. Did you choose the quotations I asked you to?"

"Yeah, I got a good one from *Crime and Punishment*. My mother wrote it out. It's in the drawer, in the back, in my notebook. Want to get it?"

Ann opened the drawer and reached for the notebook. "Is this it? Page 230. 'Pain and suffering are always inevitable for a large intelligence and a deep heart.' Think that's true?"

"I guess so."

"What this?" She held up a pink foam hair curler that was lying in the drawer.

"Oh, that. Dottie's teaching me something. You'll appreciate it, when I can do it right."

"What?"

"Writing."

"Writing—using this? How? May I see?"

"I can't do it yet."

"Let me see you try."

"I need a bed tray and pen and paper—too much trouble, Ms. Treer."

"I'll get everything together for you if you'll show me."

"Must I?"

She nodded. "Come on, if you can write, you can send messages to Diane. Sealed. *Personal*."

"O.K., O.K. Don't expect much, though. The bed tray's over there. Got a felt pen? And something to write on?"

She put the bed tray in front of him and took a pen and a sheet of paper from her briefcase.

"O.K.," he said. "Force the pen through the hole in the middle of the foam curler. See, with the foam around the pen it'll stay between my fingers, maybe." He raised his arms and rested them on the tray.

"This is ingenious. Where does the pen go?" she asked.

"Between my second and third fingers. My thumb's no good."

She jammed the foam cylinder between his fingers so that it stuck securely and the tip of the pen touched the paper.

"The pen's staying now," he said. "Last time it kept dropping. See, all the action's got to come from my shoulder." He made a wobbly line on the paper. "Hey, I'm doing it. That's an *I*, in case you can't tell. What should I write?"

"Write her a note."

"Write to Diane?"

"Yes. Write her a message and I'll take it to her."

"Man, Ms. Treer . . ."

"Make it short—*Guiness Book of World Records*—shortest letter ever written."

He sighed. She saw his face contort as he made a down-stroke, up, down, up.

"W?" she asked.

"Yeah."

The foam cylinder held firm. She watched him make an A—wavy, oversized—then a slanting N, a T. "You're writing! Go on, finish!"

"You'll take it to her after the lesson?"

"On my way home. How's that? This is great, Gary. By the time I see you at Phillips you'll be writing in your journal. Go ahead. You've got it now." She read from the paper . . . " 'I WANT' . . . Go on, Gary."

He concentrated, lifted his elbow. "Tell her how hard this was, O.K.?" Gary said. "I mean, so she doesn't say, 'Why didn't he write more?' Here goes, shortest letter ever written." His shoulder moved.

Ann followed the tip of the pen with her eyes. "I WANT 2 C U," she read, the letters running downhill. "Great, Gary. You're writing! I'll take it to her. She'll be so happy. *I'm* so happy!" she said, touching his arm. "O.K., now . . . let's get on with the lesson."

chapter **15**

She'd better get moving if she was going to make it to Phillips on time in Friday traffic. Ann, stuffing her test papers and the yearbook photographs for Gary into her briefcase, went to the closet for her coat.

"Ms. Treer . . .? Oh, I was so afraid you left! Hi." Diane laid her books down. "I wrote to Gary, and I thought you could take it with you."

"Sure." Ann put on her coat. "You just caught me."

"Would it be O.K. if I call you tonight, Ms. Treer, to see how he is?"

"Sure. Fine."

Diane, handing her the envelope, leaned against a desk.

"You haven't seen him either, since he went to Phillips, have you?"

"No. This'll be my first time there. He sent me a tape, you know, as an assignment—describing everything. It's very interesting. That reminds me . . ." Ann took the cassette out of the desk drawer and put it in her coat pocket.

"Gary told me about the tape," Diane said. "He called me Tuesday. He wasn't too sure if he liked Phillips when I spoke to him. What do you think—does he like it?"

"Oh, about as well as I'd expect," Ann said. "It's a big change."

"I know. He said there are a lot of people there who are really bad off. I hope he doesn't get depressed, Ms. Treer."

"He's too busy."

"Yeah, he says they don't treat you at all like you're sick. If you sit around and expect to be waited on, they just look at you."

"That'll be good for him in the long run."

"I guess so," Diane said. "I worry, though. I think he's lonely. I could hear it in his voice. But you know *him*. He wouldn't admit it."

"It's going to take time." Ann buttoned her coat.

Diane nodded. "I wish I could see him."

"Can't you get a ride over the weekend?"

"Not from my parents. I could call the Maddens, but I feel funny."

"There's nobody else?"

"Not this weekend. Billy's got a car, but he's got a game tomorrow."

"Well, if you're stuck, I'll take you out one of these days when I'm not tutoring."

"That'd be fantastic. You don't know how terrible it is, not seeing him. There's not even a bus that goes out there."

"We'll figure it out." Ann turned off the lights. "Where are you off to?" she asked.

"Color-guard practice, for tomorrow." Diane gathered her books and edged toward the door. "I still haven't gotten over last week's game, Ms. Treer. Losing by one point! I feel so sorry for Buck. The guys on the team said he was really broken up."

"Yes, he had his mind set on winning it." Ann picked up her briefcase. "O.K., then, Diane, so I'll be hearing from you. . . ."

" 'Bye, Ms. Treer. Tell Gary I'll write a long letter and I'll visit as soon as I can."

Ann, carrying her briefcase and tape recorder, walked down the dark corridor to the parking-lot exit. School deserted on a Friday, as usual. Except for the coaches, out there working overtime. Buck had taken his loss hard. They'd blown their perfect season.

She went to her car, and while the motor was warming up, she put the cassette in the recorder. Then she pulled out of the lot and headed for River Drive. Traffic was heavy. No wonder no other tutor would take Fridays. When the worst congestion was past, she hit the *play* button of the recorder.

"Hello, Ms. Treer. This is coming to you live from PIR, Phillips Institute of Rehabilitation. . . ."

Gary's voice was clear but unnatural, younger sounding than in real life. She turned up the volume.

"I don't know where to begin, Ms. Treer. First I have to get used to talking into this thing. The nurse plugged it in for me, and she went out of the room, so I'm by myself. This side runs thirty minutes, I think. I'll have to say a lot to fill all that.

"I'm sitting in my chair—my wheelchair—right now, in

this little room, not my regular bedroom, because I didn't want my roommates bugging me while I do this. O.K., I may as well start with my roommates. Tommy. You already know Tommy. He was rooming with José and Howie, but he asked to be in with me and they let him switch. The other two guys in our room are Drew Hutchins and David Kearns. Drew's about twenty-five, twenty-six. He was going to pick up his wife one night, and his car crashed into a train, and now he's a double amputee. One leg below the knee, one at the thigh. He's not shy—he'll show anybody what it looks like. They say around here that the big thing is your attitude. Drew's got a good attitude. Always talking about his wife and how good-looking she is and about how she's going to help him get started in a business of his own when he gets out of here. I saw her last night. She is good-looking."

There was a crackle on the tape. Ann honked her horn, passed the car ahead of her. Gary's voice returned, an undertone.

"O.K., next David. David Kearns. He's a nineteen-year-old quadriplegic with a neck injury higher up than mine, and he can't do much for himself. He's the quietest guy I ever met. I'm often quiet, too, so I'm not putting him down for that, but this guy is . . . well, he hasn't told anybody anything—not anything about where he comes from, or his family, or how he got injured. The rumor is he hit his head diving, and that his parents are loaded. They never come to visit, but supposedly on weekends they send some male nurse here to get him. Drew told me the parents built David his own house on their property so he can be taken care of but they won't have to look at him. David Kearns interests me in a weird way. I might try talking to him.

"Anyway, those are my roommates. I'll come back to them later. I have a feeling this isn't going to be too well organized, Ms. Treer. I'm just rambling. Next I'm going to talk about my first day—leaving the hospital and coming in the ambulance, and seeing this place. That was Monday. I've been here three days now. Monday they got me up real early at St. Agnes and Dr. Kimball came to say good-bye. He told me my doctor here would be Dr. Roth. Dr. Susan Roth. A woman doctor. Frankly—and I hope you don't think I'm putting women down, Ms. Treer—I wasn't too hot on having a woman doctor, but Kimball said she's highly respected, plus they don't give you a choice, so what could I do? The medical director is Dr. Greenstone. He comes around and asks everybody how they are every morning, and they all say fine and he goes away. Maybe that's all he does, I don't know.

"So anyway, back to St. Agnes. . . . Sister Marie dressed me—I'm wearing clothes, finally. And my parents packed my cards and clippings and tapes and everything, and at the last minute I felt kind of strange, like I didn't want to leave. Crazy, after waiting and waiting to get out of there. . . . Dottie came and said good-bye and kissed me, and my mother gave everybody presents, and it was a real *thing*. I felt like I ought to be getting a diploma or something. . . ."

Ann turned onto the parkway and stopped to pay a quarter at the toll booth.

"Hope I'm not boring you with all this, Ms. Treer. . . . After that they carried me out on a stretcher to the ambulance—my second ambulance ride in two months. New Bridge Volunteer Ambulance Corps. My parents came with me, and the whole way my mother kept giving me this rap about how nice the setting at Phillips is. 'Just like a country club,' she kept saying. Sure, Ma, where's the golf course? Oh, yeah, the ambulance driver blew the siren once, just for the hell of it. I forgot to say this before, but the biggest kick coming out of St. Agnes was breathing air. I mean *outside air*. I was breathing like a maniac.

"So then we got here about ten A.M. I have to admit, the place does look pretty good. Modern brick building with a sort of courtyard in the middle. Lots of trees outside—evergreens, I guess, since it's winter. It was cold, though, and gray. Man, next week's Thanksgiving already.

"Then Dr. Roth met us at the admissions office and took me to my room. Almost everybody's got a stereo and a TV with remote control. Everything's clean in this place, I'll say that. They keep disinfecting all the time with a thing like a fire extinguisher. Dr. Roth took my parents and me—in my chair—around to all the departments. Physical therapy—PT—that's a big gym where you work out on mats. Occupational therapy—OT—you do crafts and other stuff there, that're supposed to help your different muscles. In ADL—activities of daily living—they teach you how to get along when you leave—shaving, buttoning your clothes, washing, all like that. Soon I'll be able to shave myself with the electric razor Diane gave me. Let's see, they also have pre-vocational. That's supposed to prepare you for a job. I didn't go there yet.

"And then there's the psychology department. That one I don't dig too much. A weird thing happened when they took me in there. Dr. Roth told me, 'This is John Vacaro, our psychologist.' I looked at this other guy in a wheelchair and said, 'Where?' The guy said, 'Right here, man, I'm John.' So—well, that was a surprise. So we rapped for a while, and he wasn't too bad. He got injured in sports, too—wrestling, about twelve years ago. He wanted to be an airplane pilot, he said, but he likes what he does here, says flying sounds boring to him now. He's married and has a kid.

"Hey, Ms. Treer, guess I'm not such a quiet guy after all. Man, I didn't realize there was so much to tell. Here goes again. There're so many weird contraptions people have around here, you wouldn't believe. David Kearns has one of those breath-powered wheelchairs. He sips into a pipe to go forward and blows into it for reverse. On his bed he's got this electronic thing to call the nurse and turn on TV and a bunch of other stuff, also by sipping. Gordy's got these steel and leather braces and Drew's got fake legs—prostheses. Me, they put a little thing called a C-clip on my wrist that can hold a fork or a toothbrush. José has a cardholder for playing poker, and another guy holds a cigarette with a fork attached to his C-clip. Everybody's got a gadget. I'm still wearing my neck brace, of course. When that comes off, I can wheel right into a shower in my chair. Man, a shower! And go home for a visit. Home. Dr. Roth says it might not be for two more months. So I'll be stuck here without getting out for Christmas and New Year's and longer. . . .

"Oh, yeah, speaking of Dr. Roth, she and these other specialists gave me a complete evaluation when I came on Monday. She told me afterward most of the same stuff Kimball said before. My injury's around the two lowest neck bones. 'What chance do you think I have to walk?' I asked her when she was done. 'Can't give you a percentage on miracles,' she said. 'How about a five percent chance?' I said. I figured she'd say, 'Sure, at least!' She just laughed, like it wasn't a serious question. Guess I'm gonna have to show her *and* Kimball what's what."

The tape faded out. Ann moved into the right-hand lane,

slowed for the exit ramp. She took a left onto Briar Road. After a pause she heard Gary's voice again.

"I don't know yet how I feel about Dr. Roth. She's O.K., I guess. I think she tries a little too hard to act important so you won't forget she's a doctor. The therapists aren't like that at all—real friendly. Ben Robie's assigned to me, same one Tommy has. Ben's an ex-soccer player. A big, calm guy with a Jamaican accent. Sounds like he ought to be doing radio commercials . . . 'Come to Jamaica' . . . 'Buy herbal shampoo' . . . like that. All in all, the staff's good. No complaints.

"You must be wondering how I feel about the whole place, Ms. Treer. I guess it sounds pretty good from what I've been saying—modern, good staff, no complaints. But— I don't know if I should say this—hell, why not?—I feel like an oddball here, I really do. I'm not going to go around telling that to anybody, but this tape is private, right? I can say whatever I think? If anybody wants you to hand over the evidence, Ms. Treer, chew it up and swallow it, promise?

"So anyway, about feeling like an oddball. I think it's because of all the wrecked-up and wacked-out people here. I mean, I thought Tommy was putting me on with his stories, but the stuff he told me was probably all true. Howie, for instance, was born with cerebral palsy. He's all doubled up. He's always got a radio in his lap, knows the words to every song in the top forty. Everybody mocks him out. José's the religious kid. He fell off a ladder and thinks he got reborn. He can't even move as much as David Kearns. Then there's Gordy Jonas. He's a paraplegic who's always sneaking in booze and organizing wheelchair races. And a kid whose name I don't know, who has brain damage. He can't say words, but he can spell T-O-I-L-E-T when he has to go. I swear to God, I heard him yesterday and I couldn't help laughing. You know why? I was sitting there thinking, 'Treer ought to teach that kid anagrams.' Think I'm getting wacked-out, too, Ms. Treer?"

Ann followed the sign up the hill to Phillips.

"Wait a minute . . . wait a minute . . . I was just kidding about that. I'm O.K., honest. The patients here are nice—really. Drew's a good guy—very together. And there's a girl named Liz who was born with something wrong with her spine, but she's very smart. The other guys think she's stuck-up, but hell, that's because she shows them up. She's got this terrific attitude. That's the only thing. Everybody here says so. If your attitude's good, you'll make it. I was . . . exaggerating before about that oddball stuff. In fact, I'm getting sort of a reputation around here already for working hard and having a good attitude.

"Let's see, what else? I've had visitors. Buck and Wally came up last night, and my parents, naturally. . . . Can't wait to see Diane. . . ."

Ann pushed the *off* button and drove along the tree-lined roadway into the parking lot. Lights were lit at Phillips now that the sun had gone down. She parked the car and gathered her books. At the entrance, wide, electric-eye doors opened to admit her.

"Gary Madden," she said to the receptionist.

"You can go right to his room, number 110."

She walked down the hall past curtained doorways. A patient in a wheelchair smiled at her. A pleasant place that felt more like a school than a hospital. Room 110. She knocked.

"Come in."

It was Gary's voice. She stepped inside.

"Hi," he said. "Did you find the place O.K.?"

"Oh, sure," she said, "I feel as if I've been here before."

146

chapter 16

"Get the aide to wheel you in, Gary," Tommy said. "We got a traffic tie-up."

Gary yawned as the aide pushed him into the physical therapy department. Two weeks at Phillips and he was worn out. Not that he was complaining to anybody.

"A little further yet," Tommy called. "Make room for Gordy, and here comes Father José. How goes it, Padre? Give us a blessing, man?"

José, sipping into the tube, manuevered his chair. "I bless you all the time. You don't have to ask me."

"Hey, you guys," Tommy glanced over his shoulder toward the double doors, "where's the staff? Where's Ben Robie? They tell you to come to PT at nine sharp in the morning, and then all's they do is make you wait. You pay good money to come to this place, and what do you get?"

"Bedsores," Gordy said.

"What's your hurry?" José asked.

"I'm *walking* today, that's my hurry."

Gary looked at Tommy. "Your braces came?"

"Yeah."

"Great. What kind?" Gordy asked. "Sand-blasted finish?"

"No, hell, no," Tommy said. "I like my chrome polished, nice and shiny."

"How much did they set you back?" Gordy asked.

"Nine hundred fifty-nine seventy-five. The best, man, the best. I studied every catalogue. What'd yours cost you?"

"Eight."

"Eight hundred? Is that all? You got a box-type joint with drop lock?"

"No, I don't need that."

"Toe pickup assist unit?"

"Naa."

Tommy lit a cigarette. "Well, then you ain't got the best. Nine hundred fifty-nine seventy-five. That's what mine set me back. Wait til you see the leatherwork. . . ."

Gary yawned again. He felt like sliding out of his chair and sacking out for a while instead of spending two hours on the mats, and balancing and going up on the tilt table. Hadn't slept too well the last couple of nights. Those dreams again. In the one he was trying to carry a heavy sack, but it always fell off his shoulder or ripped open or made him trip. And in the other one . . . couldn't remember it too well, but something about it had bugged him. Let's see, how was it . . . a giant turtle chasing him. . . .

Gary's eyes wandered around the room. Liz was down on a mat already, lifting a sandbag weight, even before her therapist got her started. Tommy and Gordy were yakking about their hotshot braces. José was praying.

"Lookit Liz," Gordy said. "Eager beaver."

Tommy blew out smoke. "I can't take that chick. She thinks she's tough shit. College girl."

"What's wrong with that?" Gary said.

Tommy snorted. "Hey, man," he said suddenly, "you know your leg's moving?"

Gary looked first at Tommy, then at his leg. Holy hell. He felt the vibrations. His right leg was doing a little dance, sticking out straight. What had Roth said to him—she wouldn't give a percentage on miracles? Damn it, he'd show Roth a thing or two about percentages. *His legs were coming back!*

"Is that your first one?" Gordy asked.

"One?" Gary said. Everybody was watching him.

"Spasm, buddy," Tommy said. "Your first spasm."

"Naa, I've had 'em," Gary said uncertainly. A spasm. That's all it was. As spinal shock wore off he'd get them, Roth had said. Everybody did. Howie's spasms threw him out of his chair sometimes.

"Get Ben to do your knee when he comes," Gordy said.

"When Ben comes, he's taking me first," Tommy said, mashing out his cigarette.

"No, I'm not." Ben came up behind Tommy's chair and wheeled him to the mats. "I'm starting Gary first, and I'm sending you over to get your braces on. I'll be over later. Go, man, you're going to walk! O.K., Gary, let's hit the mat."

Gary raised his arms so that Ben could lift him out of the chair and lower him.

149

"You had a spasm just now?" Ben asked.

"Yeah. It's gone."

"If they bother you, tell Dr. Roth, you hear? She can order you something—medication. I'm going to bend your knee, like this . . . and do the range of motion. . . ."

Gary felt himself being pulled forward, his neck brace chafing slightly. Keep talking, Ben, he thought. Sell me some plane tickets, sell me shampoo. . . . Ben's voice made sandy beaches appear in his head, and girls with long, clean hair. Diane? Hey, Diane . . . send a letter with Ms. Treer when she comes, O.K.? Can't wait to see you. Diane was coming Saturday, for sure. Treer was bringing her.

"Now your left leg," Ben was saying. "You're doing fine, you know, Gary, because you're an athlete. That's a big advantage. Some of these old folks, they don't have that going for them."

"I know."

"I'm going to cut this short and put you up on the table," Ben said. "I've got to go help Tommy. Jack, give me a hand," he called.

Two guys to manage one, Gary thought, as they lifted him into his wheelchair. Ben strapped him, released the brake, and pushed him to the tilt table where they lifted and strapped again. Ben padded him with pillows and raised his head.

"I'll be back," Ben said.

Well, here he was, strapped, trapped, deserted. Good. A little peace. So Tommy was going to walk. He wasn't even envious. Up here on the table at least he could rest. Could sleep, maybe, except that the sun was streaming through the vertical venetian blinds into his eyes. He squinted as he looked down on Liz, lifting and balancing, and on Gordy by the parallel bars. Everybody was busy. José, on the plinth, was getting stretched. Drew was walking with his prostheses. David Kearns—well, he wasn't exactly busy. Lying there on the mat, staring at the ceiling, his skinny hands turned awkwardly into his chest. Weird, Gary thought as he looked over the room, that he'd never known a single disabled person before he got here. Where had they been, in hiding? A couple of them—that lady who never stopped crying or old Mr. Filippi, who was grunting under a two-pound weight—you couldn't help thinking, was it worth the trouble—the staff's—their own?

"Hey, dig it!"

Gary watched. Tommy, a crutch under each arm, was being supported at the waist by Ben Robie. The metal shafts of his braces gleamed in the sun. Ben let go, and Tommy swayed. Pinocchio, Gary thought. Once he'd had a wooden Pinocchio toy, with legs like Tommy's were now —rigid as skinny trees.

"Ready . . ." Ben said, "get set . . . go!"

Tommy lunged. He swung the crutches forward and pulled his wooden-toy legs up even. A crazy hop and slide.

"I walked!" he shouted. "I walked a fuckin' step!" He raised the crutches off the floor and teetered for a second before they dropped from his hands. Ben grabbed him too late and he sprawled on his face.

Drew cheered. Liz applauded. Ben, picking Tommy up, patted his behind. Gary watched, dazed by the sunlight. So that was walking. Walking for Tommy, maybe. He had some other ideas about walking, himself. He closed his eyes to shield them from the glare. Oh, man, what drowsiness! Take a nap. He dozed. That dream last night—the one that had been bugging him. The memory of it was coming back . . . a turtle. . . . He remembered now. A giant turtle had opened its mouth, ready to swallow him,

and he had done the only thing he could—snarled at it—
and it had slunk away. Now he understood what was different. No chase, like in most dreams. No great escape. A first
for him. In his tortoise dream he had been paralyzed.

He lay with his eyes closed, losing track of time.

"Should he come down?"

What was that, a voice in his head?

"Who?"

"That quad."

Gary opened his eyes and turned as far as his neck brace
would allow. Two girls, student therapists, were standing
near him.

"Which quad?" one whispered.

"That one on the table."

Quad. Who were they talking about, anyway? He looked
at the tilt table on his left, the one on his right. One, two,
three tilt tables. Suddenly his head bumped something
hard, and with the bump came a flash of understanding. It
was only the pillow behind his head that had slipped to the
floor, but it seemed, in his confusion, as if the heavy sack
of his dreams had fallen again and was bringing him down
with it.

chapter **17**

"Superquad!"

Gary watched a wheelchair zip past his room. Gordy Jonas again, yelling that at him. Treer, just finishing the lesson, looked up. "It was Gordy," he said, "the kid in the next room."

"The one who organizes races?"

"Yeah. He calls me Superquad." Sounded weird, saying the name himself. Gary studied his hands that lay palms down on the tray of his wheelchair. "Gordy—some of the others, too—they needle me—say I'm trying to be, you know, a superhero, best patient, win boy-scout points, stuff like that."

"Are you?"

He waited to answer. No, damn it, he wasn't trying to be anything. That's just the way he was. That's the way he'd played football and the way he was playing it now. "I'm not trying to make them look bad," he said finally. "Just working, is all."

"And it's paying off, isn't it?"

"Oh, yeah. You should see—I'm getting good at sitting balance. Ben sits me up, and an aide stands behind to make sure I don't topple over. Then Ben pushes me a little and I have to try to resist. Like blocking in football, except I'm learning to sit—crazy." Later he'd have to show her his newest bit. She got a kick out of hearing about this stuff.

"And you're feeding yourself, right?"

"Yeah. A little messy, but I'm getting there. They put a guard around the plate so the food doesn't get pushed off."

"Has your mother seen you do it?"

"Yes, I showed her last night."

"Has she seen you balance?"

"She gets nervous."

"Diane'll be thrilled to see what you've learned."

"Yeah, you're bringing her out this Saturday, right?"

"Yes."

"Thanks a lot. I really appreciate that."

Ms. Treer leaned back in her seat. "How do you feel about that nickname?" she asked.

"Superquad?" Gary glanced at the door. Everybody'd be coming back to the room soon before supper. He'd have to explain fast. "Uh—it doesn't faze me. You know, 'Sticks and stones may break my bones . . .'"

"Maybe," Treer said. "But names can hurt sometimes."

"Yeah, well, to tell you the truth, at first I didn't appreciate *Superquad* too much," he said. "Like in school, most people don't want to stand out. They want to be like everybody else, not super. And then *quad*. I hated how that sounded at first. To me it sounded like *freak*. But you get used to it—para, quad—just abbreviations. The staff, when somebody has pretty good abilities for his level and is really working, they say he's a good quad. Superquad's just a joke, but I'd like to be a good quad. I would. No, the nickname doesn't bother me."

"Good," she said. "Say, don't I still have an assignment to give you?"

"Yeah. Finish the play by Ibsen?"

"Yes, and answer this question on *Death of a Salesman*. Why does Willy kill himself?"

"Because he lost his job, right?" Gary said. "Because nobody respected him anymore. What else is there to say?"

"Consider his suicide as an act of love, an act of self-sacrifice."

"Act of love?"

"Yes, and one more thing for your journal," Ann said. "Think of a metaphor for your life."

"Metaphor . . . that's a comparison without 'as' or 'like'?"

"Yes. A teacher gave me that assignment once, and I always remembered it."

"What was your metaphor?" Gary asked.

"Swimming—you know I'm a swimming nut, right? I wrote that I wanted my life to be a good swim—going a long distance with grace and apparent ease even in the face of drowning."

"Yeah? Have you done it?"

"Almost drowned? Lots of times."

"No, I mean the grace and ease."

She smiled. "I'm still trying."

Gary looked up. A chair rolled through the doorway,

motor whirring. End of privacy. The other guys would all be heading back to the room now. David was first. David Kearns with his eyes straight ahead. Gary opened his mouth to say hi. Hell, what was the use? He'd been saying it and getting no answer. He watched as David, sipping into the tube, moved his chair to the other side of the room where he faced the wall.

"He always does that," Gary whispered to Treer so that she had to read his lips. "He just sits there until the nurse takes him to dinner."

They heard a clunk of metal on metal. Drew and Tommy were trying to come through the doorway, both at the same time. Drew fended off Tommy with his arm and pulled in first.

"Best man won again," Drew said.

Tommy thumped on the back of Drew's chair. "Screw you, man."

"Hey, Superquad!" Drew saluted Gary. "Oh, sorry, didn't know you had company." Drew swung his chair around and faced Ann. "I don't believe we've met," he said. "I'm Drew Hutchins."

Gary, listening to the introductions, looked at the pinned bottoms of Drew's pants legs. Hey, Drew, *put your best foot forward*, he felt like saying. Why the hell did that expression pop into his head? Sick! No, not sick. No sicker than Superquad. What would Drew do if he said that? Get mad? Laugh? He wasn't sure, just as he wasn't sure what *he* was going to do sometimes when they called him Superquad. Were words harmless, like Tommy thought, or could they hurt, like Treer had just finished saying? And if they hurt, what were you supposed to do around this place when you didn't like what somebody said to you? You sure as hell couldn't haul off and slug them.

Tommy wheeled over to his bed. "Hey, Tom," Gary called, "this is Ms. Treer. Remember you met her at St. Agnes?"

"Yeah. Hullo."

Drew was rattling away a mile a minute to Treer. ". . . so that's why I didn't graduate from college," he was telling her, "but I'll probably go back and pick up those business courses when I get out of here."

Confident S.O.B. Had he been like that before his accident? Gary wondered. He'd been thinking about that a lot these days. Had José always been religious? Had Tommy always been a reckless nut? And what about David Kearns?

"How long have you been here?" Ms. Treer was asking Drew.

"Five months, one week, and three days."

"And how have you found it?"

"The best—the best—Ann, is it?"

"Yes."

"The best, Ann. Linda—my wife—she checked out all the rehab places and sold me on Phillips."

Ann, Gary thought. Drew sure got acquainted fast. Ann. Did she have any nicknames? he wondered.

"Phillips is realistic," Drew was saying. "Some rehab institutes coddle you, and some treat you unbelievably rough —you know, survival of the fittest: Fend for yourself, cripple, *out there* nobody's going to take care of you! But Phillips is middle of the road. That's what I like about it. They treat you nice, but they don't baby you."

"They sure as hell don't," Tommy said, lighting up a cigarette.

Gary looked at each one of them in turn—Tommy taking a long drag on his butt, Drew grinning at Treer, Treer listening politely, David staring at the wall. One of the nurses was coming in now to get David. It looked like David was saying something to her as she followed him out of the room.

Tommy exhaled a cloud of smoke. "Whew!" he said when David was gone. "Don't he spook you out?"

"Dr. Greenstone ought to do something about him," Drew said. "Somebody ought to *make* him talk."

"Maybe he was a loner before his accident," Gary said.

Drew shifted in his chair. "Then make him change! Nobody has to be alone in this place."

"I don't think . . . you can change a person," Gary said. He looked at Treer. She was concentrating, resting her chin on her hand. "What do you think?" he asked her.

"Well," she said, "they say your personality's formed by the time you're five or six years old. Some say earlier. I think the way you handle an accident or illness or anything must depend on your personality before it happened, and on how your family and friends take it."

"Naa, it's all luck," Tommy said, flicking an ash. "What does it matter what the kid was like before, or how his parents are—with a guy like Kearns, I mean? Look at his level—high up in his neck. Rotten luck! That's all. He can't do nothing!"

"José's about the same level," Drew said, "and look at him—he's one of the happiest guys here."

Tommy sniffed. "He's crazy, too."

"Come on, Tommy," Gary said. "I don't go for that reborn stuff either, but it helps José. He's got a great attitude. Have you ever seen him play poker, praying for a good hand? Have you watched him type with a pencil in his mouth?"

"Yeah, I've seen it." Tommy lit another cigarette. "Still in all, if I were in José's shoes . . ."

"Yeah?" Drew said. "What would you do?"

The room was silent. Tommy chuckled softly. "I'd—I'd stay high. Or sleep all the time, like Cominski."

"I thought you were going to say something else," Gary said.

Tommy hunched. "Yeah, well, there's that, too. Somebody might help you O.D."

"So you'd give up," Drew said. "You'd quit."

"Quit what? That's living?" Tommy laughed. "That—what Kearns has got—vroom, vroom, suck in your breath and hit one mile an hour—that's *living?*"

"It's living if you think it is," Gary said. "You'd still have your head, right?" Sounded like something Treer would say. Maybe she had.

"Your head." Tommy smirked. "Remember what I used to tell you at St. A's? You're too much for the head, Superquad. Too much *for words.*" He looked at Treer uncertainly. "I always used to be telling him that."

Gary watched the corners of Tommy's lips curl in a smile. "My head's everything," he said quietly, though he felt as if his temperature was rising. Damn it, he was annoyed. Pissed off. "Attitude's *everything.*" Their eyes were on him now—everybody's. Did they expect him to say something else, do something? "I'll show you," he said suddenly, feeling like a little kid, bragging, picking a fight. "I'll show you attitude's everything. Want proof?"

Treer was leaning forward. Don't worry, Treer. I won't make a jerk of myself. He straightened his shoulders, brushed his adhesive cuffs against the wheels. "Want proof?" he repeated.

"What? What proof?" Tommy asked.

"I can't wheel my chair yet, right?"

"Right."

"O.K.," he said, "mind over matter. I'm going to wheel

myself to . . . the door, just by *willing* it, by *wanting* to do it."

"Hoax!" Tommy called.

Tommy was trying to make a joke of it. O.K., let him. Maybe it was one.

"Gary?" Treer was nervous.

"Phony!" Tommy said.

"O.K.," Gary shook his shoulders. "I'm willing myself to that door. Get ready . . . get set . . ." He built up friction between his cuff and the lug on the wheel. "Go!" He pushed. The chair rolled, he pushed again and still again until he reached the door. He had his back to them, so he couldn't see their faces.

"Gary," he heard Treer say.

"Attitude!" Drew called. "Let's hear it for attitude!"

"Hoax!" Tommy said.

Gary smiled. Tommy was right, actually. He'd wheeled to the door earlier in the afternoon, but they didn't have to know that, did they? "Mind over matter!" he said. Too bad he couldn't turn the chair around. He'd like to see their faces.

Tommy let out a long, low whistle. "Yeah, Superquad!"

"Thank you, thank you," Gary said. Hell, he might as well play it up. He was what he was.

chapter **18**

"Are we almost there, Ms. Treer?"

"It's not far. We get off at exit 35." Ann pressed on the horn and skirted around the car in front of her.

"I appreciate the ride," Diane said. "You were coming out here anyway?"

"Well, let's say it's no trouble. I wanted Gary to have a certain book, and I'm free until this evening."

"You're going out tonight?"

"Yes."

"That's nice." Diane pulled nervously at the earring in her newly pierced ear.

"Gary's parents are coming out to Phillips today, too,

aren't they?" Ann asked. She rolled down her window to drop a quarter in the toll box, and a puff of fog blew in.

"Yes, and his aunt, all the way from Wisconsin," Diane said. "All Gary's relatives live out there."

"I know. Which aunt is this?"

"Evelyn, her name is. His mother's sister. They're going to the airport to pick her up before they come out. She's staying til New Year's. Can you believe it's only three weeks until Christmas, Ms. Treer? It's sure going to be a strange Christmas this year."

"I know."

"Gary'll be at Phillips—who knows if I'll even be with him Christmas Day. . . ." Diane squirmed and sat on one foot. "I couldn't sleep last night, Ms. Treer. I was so nervous about seeing him. I still am. This last week's been almost as bad as the week of the accident."

"You mean because of your job?"

"Not only that. The job was too much for me anyway, so it's almost good they let me go. I won't be able to buy a car, but . . ." She shrugged. "No, it's not the job. It's this —this not knowing exactly how Gary wants me to be."

"I guess you'll just have to be yourself."

"I'm *trying*," she said. "But lately people are really getting to me. My parents—I told you my mother wouldn't like the idea of my going to college with Gary, didn't I? Well, I was right. And my parents aren't the only ones acting strange toward me, either."

"Who else?"

"Oh, a lot of kids. Boys, especially," she said. "I haven't gone out with anyone. I don't think I would, even if they asked me. But the thing is, I don't have to worry about it, because nobody'll ask."

"How do you know?"

"I can tell. They wouldn't do that to Gary. They think I'm Gary's. To them, I'm like a—"

"A widow?" Ann asked.

"Yes," Diane said, folding her arms. "But I don't care. I am Gary's, in a way."

Ann slowed down as she hit another patch of fog. "Well, Gary's accident changed a lot of things for a lot of people. Everybody's still adjusting."

"I know," Diane said. "*That day* . . . I try not to, but I keep thinking about that day, about why couldn't Gary have been taken out just before that play, or why couldn't the guy he tackled have got past him and run all the way for a touchdown? I dream about it, Ms. Treer. I have these dreams where I wake up shaking. I say to myself, God must've wanted it that way, but. . . ." She shook her head.

Ann switched gears and turned up the hill. "I know what you mean," she said.

Diane looked out the window. "I hope I have a chance to see him alone before his family gets here. Is that Phillips, up there?"

"Yes." They wound through the tract of evergreens and into the parking lot.

"It looks like a school," Diane said. "I pictured it—I don't know—looking like a castle up here in the hills."

Ann turned off the motor. They got out of the car and walked toward the entrance. The electric-eye doors opened for them.

Diane looked up and down the hall.

"I'll show you where Gary's room is," Ann said, "and then I'm going down to the lounge for a while."

"Thanks," Diane whispered. "It's so quiet here, Ms. Treer!"

"A lot of patients go home weekends."

The heels of their shoes squeaked on the waxed floor of the corridor.

"This is it," Ann said. "Gary's room."

"Ms. Treer, I'm nervous." Her voice was faint.

"You—you look great." Ann squeezed Diane's arm. "Go on in, he's waiting."

"Somebody's in there with him, Ms. Treer."

"That's O.K. Go in."

Diane walked tentatively through the doorway.

Ann paused for a second and walked slowly toward the lounge. At the end of the hall she heard a sound behind her. She turned around.

"Excuse me—Ann Treer?" A young man in a wheelchair pulled up alongside her.

"Yes?"

"Hi, I'm John Vacaro, the psychologist working with Gary."

"Oh, yes."

"I was in his room just now when his girl friend came. He's been telling me about you. He told me you were bringing Diane out today. Nice to meet you. I just wanted to say hello."

"It's good to meet you, too." She paused. "How's Gary doing?"

"Do you have a minute?" John asked. "Come have a cup of coffee in my office."

"Sure, I'd like to."

John, wheeling his chair, led the way. "I always like to get a chance to talk to the people closest to my patients," he said. "Here. Turn right. This is it."

Ann opened the door, waited for him to go through the doorway first.

"How do you like your coffee?" John asked, approaching a low table with a hotplate on it.

"No sugar, please. Milk if you have it." Should she offer to fix it?

John set out two cups and, holding the pot handle with both hands, poured the coffee. "Would you get the milk from the refrigerator there, behind you? Thanks. Please sit down."

She sat on a straight-backed chair opposite him.

"There, help yourself," John said. He picked up a cup. "Gary's a good kid, isn't he?"

"Yes. I'm really fond of him."

John nodded. "Do you feel the tutoring's going well?"

"Yes," she said. "He's doing everything I ask him to. It's hard for him to keep up with the reading, but he does it, and he's really surprised me with his writing. In class I never got the impression he was that interested in writing, but now—well, that's been a nice surprise."

"Does he write about the accident, about his feelings?"

"He's beginning to. A little bit. And he's revealing a lot more in our talks than he did at first."

"That's great. He obviously has a lot of confidence in you." John put down his cup and wheeled behind his desk. "I'm still working on gaining his confidence."

"He's skeptical about psychologists, I think," Ann said. "At St. Agnes he didn't even want to meet the psychologist."

"I know," John said, writing a note to himself on a pad. "I know it's nothing personal. He's not the only guy around here who thinks he's a big boy and can handle this by himself. I know how it is, because I felt that way, too." He looked up. "At his age I didn't want any part of shrinks."

165

Ann smiled. "How long did it take you to become a convert?"

"A couple of years. A couple of years until I realized I wanted to join 'em instead of fight 'em. Maybe Gary won't be as stubborn as I was. I think he's smarter."

"How would you say he's doing so far?" Ann asked. "I know he works hard. He's told me other patients kid him about his determination."

"I think he's coping with the ribbing very well. He seems to get a kick out of it, actually."

"And he's getting good support from his parents, wouldn't you say?"

John hesitated. "The parents have been very cooperative. They've come in for group sessions. They're both learning a lot." He paused again. "Has Gary talked to you much about Diane?"

"Not directly, but I've gotten drawn into the middle of things without meaning to."

"How strongly do you think he feels about her?"

"I can't say for sure. He seems very attached—but scared."

John nodded. "I haven't had a chance to learn much about their relationship yet, but I know enough to detect the ambivalence there."

"What do you think he's scared of?" Ann asked. "Losing her?"

"Maybe," John said. "I'm speaking in general now, but a lot of patients fear being rejected. Let's face it, it's a realistic fear. At her age, no matter how generous Diane is, she must have some doubts about sticking with him. And it's not unusual for a patient who's afraid of being rejected to do the rejecting first, so he can always say afterward, 'She didn't dump me. It was my choice.' And then there are other things for him to be afraid of—the whole masculinity bit. I'm sure Gary wonders whether he can have a sex life. He *can*, with certain adaptations, but he doesn't seem ready to discuss that yet."

Ann put down her coffee cup. "Are you optimistic about him?"

"Guardedly," John said. "That's my outlook on most of my patients at the stage Gary's in. There's a typical pattern, you know. Naturally everybody's slightly different, but most disabled go through several stages. Shock first. Then denial. You know, 'What do you mean, this is forever? That might be true for somebody else, but not for me!' That's about where Gary is now, I think. Then usually there's an angry stage. 'Why me? It's not fair!' And a bargaining stage. 'Well, if I can just get back the use of my arms, it won't be so bad.' And then often a deep depression, before slowly getting the real picture of how things are going to be permanently. The whole thing takes time. Gary's mourning a loss. Mourning takes time."

"I know." Ann picked up her cup again. "Do some patients go into depression and never come out?"

"A few. Most of them are O.K. as long as they're here. Here everybody's in the same boat. It's leaving that's the real crunch."

"What does it depend on mostly, whether they have a good attitude or not—on how badly they were injured?"

"No, not that so much as their pre-morbid personality— what they were like before the accident—and whether they can form a new self-image that, as far as they're concerned, has worth."

"Do you think Gary'll be able to do that?"

"I hope so. Sometimes it's rougher for us athletes—us *former* athletes—to build a new self-image. Strength, body integrity, are big things to an athlete, and suddenly—poof! You can't trade on that physique anymore. It's like a beauty queen becoming hideously disfigured. What's left? you wonder. I think Gary's got more than athletics going for him, though. He seems to."

"I think he does." Ann picked up her books and moved forward on the seat. "Is there anything else you can think of that I can do for him?" she asked.

"No, just keep doing whatever you've been doing," John said. "Whatever it is, I think it's working. He's a kid who's afraid to show his feelings, his insecurities, but apparently he doesn't feel threatened by you. He's lucky to have a good teacher." He smiled. "When I think of some of the bozos *I* had. . . ."

"I see you managed O.K. in spite of them," Ann said, "which just goes to show how much influence teachers really have."

"Are you kidding? Don't discount your influence!" John wheeled his chair toward the door. "Where're you headed now, back to Gary's room?"

"Yes, I want to say hello and drop off this book."

"I'll see you as far as the cafeteria. My wife's meeting me here for lunch today."

Ann walked first through the doorway, and John swung the door shut behind them.

"How long have you worked here?" Ann asked as they went down the hall.

"Let's see, three years. I was here as a patient myself twelve years ago. How about that? Then six years in college and grad school, three working for a state agency, before this. I like Phillips. It's a good place."

"As an outsider, I'm impressed with it."

"Oh, you outsiders, you're easy to impress. Ask the patients, that's the real test."

"I have. Most of the ones I've talked to give it their seal of approval."

"We try, we try," John said, extending his hand.

Ann stepped closer and clasped it.

"Nice meeting you, Ann. Take it easy."

"You, too," she said. "I'm sure we'll see each other again." She waved, walked on, paused outside Gary's room. Voices. His parents were already here, both of them standing behind his wheelchair, looking over his shoulder. Diane was sitting next to Gary. Ann entered.

"Hey, Ms. Treer!" Gary looked up from his lapboard where there was a chessboard partly set up with oversize, lightweight pieces. "Pull up a chair," he said.

"Hello," Mr. Madden said, "I'll get chairs."

Mrs. Madden smiled. "Hello, there, Mrs. Treer. It's been a long time. . . ."

Ann sat down next to Diane as Mr. Madden arranged chairs in a circle around Gary.

"I understand you went to the airport this morning," Ann said. "Is Gary's aunt here?" she asked.

"Yes," Mrs. Madden said. She stood next to Gary with her hands on his shoulders. "My sister hasn't seen Gary yet. We just got here this minute and she stopped in the rest room."

"Thanks for the present you brought me, Ms. Treer," Gary said.

"Present? You mean the book? I haven't even given it to you yet. Here." She put it on the edge of his lapboard.

"No, I mean . . ." Gary glanced at Diane. "I mean this present here."

Diane blushed. "He's looking so good," she said. "I can't believe it."

"You gotta believe," Gary told her. "See what my dad brought me, Ms. Treer."

Ann watched him push a chesspiece into place by sliding his hand across the board.

"That's great. What're the pieces made of?"

"Balsa wood," Mr. Madden said. "Entertainment and therapy combined. He's got to put them in place by himself. Otherwise I don't take him on. How about you, Diane," he asked, "do you play chess?"

"No, I wish I could." Diane pulled on her earring.

"I'll teach you," Gary said, "if I ever get the board set up." A rook fell over, rolled onto the floor. "Damn!"

"That's all right, I've got it," Mrs. Madden bent down and picked it up. "Where does it go?"

"No helping!" Mr. Madden said.

"That's O.K., Ma, quick, while he's not looking."

Mrs. Madden put the piece in place. "The doctors here tell me the first rule for parents is 'Sit on your hands,' " she said. "I'm trying to remember, I really am. There's so much to get used to, Mrs. Treer! I'll take myself out of here and let him do it. I'll see what's keeping Evelyn. Gary, Aunt Evelyn'll be here in a minute."

"I'm not going anywhere," he said.

His mother bit in her cheeks. "Try to be . . . pleasant to Aunt Evelyn when she comes in," she said softly. "Will you try?"

Mr. Madden turned away, Ann noticed. He was looking out the window.

"I'll be charming as hell, Ma," Gary said evenly.

"I'll be back in a minute." Mrs. Madden's voice quavered.

"Look, Diane," Gary said. "Look, Ms. Treer." He had

his hand circled around the queen. "Up she goes . . ." He lifted the queen clumsily.

"That's good, Gary," Diane said.

Mr. Madden came away from the window and sat down opposite him. "Good going," he said.

Gary lifted the king. Then he raised his eyes, and paused. "Hi," he said.

Diane and Mr. Madden looked toward the door. Ann turned. Mrs. Madden and her sister stood in the doorway.

"Hi," Gary said again.

"Gary . . ." his aunt said, drawing her hand to her face. Her mouth twitched as she walked slowly toward him. Ann watched.

"Gary," his aunt repeated as she reached his chair. She put out her arms as if to embrace him, but at the last minute she pulled back and let one sob escape. "I'm so sorry, Gary," she said, hugging herself instead. "I'm so sorry— what a terrible thing!"

chapter 19

"You haven't made your move yet, have you?" Liz asked.

"No," Gary said. He slid his hand along the edge of the chessboard. "No, I was thinking." Too much, as usual, these last couple of weeks since Diane had visited. Thinking too much, considering he ought to be concentrating or Liz would cream him and give the guys something else to mock him out for. Tommy, Drew, and the boys were winding up their poker game over there on the other side of the rec room now. Visitors were gone. The recreational therapist had left for the night.

Liz leaned forward. "I just wanted to make sure I didn't miss anything. You look like you're in a trance."

"I feel like it." What was it, with all these dreams of his

lately? The one, for instance, where he was lying on his back and Diane was there, washing him with a sponge. . . . Hey, don't get thinking about that again. Liz already had his rook, knight, and two pawns.

"Shit man, a full house!" Tommy's voice went up across the room. "I'll take that pot, baby. I'll take it!"

The poker game broke up, and Tommy, jingling a bag of change, wheeled alongside Gary's chair. "Look at the two brains. How long between moves—one every five hours? Who's winning?"

"She is," Gary said.

"Jesus." Tommy, shaking his head, rolled out the door.

Drew wheeled by them. "G'night, Liz. So long, Gary."

"See you in a little while," Gary said.

José followed behind Drew. "Next time you play with us, Gary?" he asked.

"O.K. Sure." When he could hold the cards, maybe.

"God bless you, Gary, Liz," José called.

"Thanks," Gary told him. "Same to you."

"Good night," Liz said.

Gordy Jonas was the only one left now—building up speed as he crossed the room. He jumped his chair and landed again on all four wheels. "Mmmm, nighty-night!" he said. "Don't do anything I wouldn't do, Gary!"

"Don't worry." The rec room was silent. "Maybe I can pay attention to the game now," Gary said.

Liz shrugged. "We don't have to finish if you don't want to."

"I want to." He was dead tired, but he liked the quiet here better than dragging out the bedtime routine back in the room—the sponge bath, the silver bullet, as Tommy called their suppositories. Lately the bathing was getting weird. The nurse would wash him *there*, and he'd get an erection. No feeling—just a reflex action. Man, would his head and body ever work together on that? Tommy and the guys kidded around once in a while, but he didn't trust any information he got from those characters. He moved his pawn and knocked over Liz's rook. "Sorry," he said.

"That's O.K." She picked it up and made her move.

Gary studied the board. "You going home for Christmas?" he asked. Christmas in five days. Hard to believe it, even though there were decorations all over the place.

"Yes, my brother's coming for me Friday. I'll be home through New Year's."

"You're lucky. I can't go home until this neck brace comes off—another month or so."

"It shouldn't be too bad around here," she said. "Tommy's staying, isn't he?"

"Yeah, but Drew and David are going home. Drew's going for good. I guess the place'll be pretty well cleaned out."

"You'll have visitors?"

"Oh, sure. My parents are coming, and my aunt's here from Wisconsin."

"Will your girl friend be coming?" Liz asked him.

"No, she's got to be with her family, but she'll be here Christmas Eve and New Year's Eve. My English teacher's bringing her out Christmas Eve. She's bringing her and my friends Billy and Jason." He moved. "Your turn," he said.

Liz put her hand on a bishop, and paused.

Take your time, Gary thought. Man, Diane coming on Christmas Eve, another one of those daydreams that'd been haunting him. Diane wearing a white pullover . . . the two of them lying down on his bed . . . Diane taking off her sweater to be more comfortable. . . .

Liz made her move. "Have you ever been away from home at Christmas before?" she asked.

"No. Have you?"

"Oh, sure, three times in hospitals. And the last time, you know what really got to me? The nurses brought everybody a cupcake with a little candy cane sticking in it. That candy cane is what freaked me out. It was so *pathetic*. I cried."

"You're laughing now," he said. Weird, she hardly ever did. Serious girl. Nice-looking, with fine hair like a little kid's. Looked like a kid, in fact, even though she was twenty.

"Well, it's ridiculous, isn't it? I mean, if you have to cry, there are plenty of things more pathetic than a candy cane on Christmas."

"I can't picture you crying at all."

"Good." She fiddled with one of the chesspieces.

Jesus, he thought, if anybody had reason to cry it was her. She'd never walked in her life.

"Go on," she said.

He edged his pawn onto a space with one of hers.

"Take my pawn," she said.

"I did."

"I mean *take* it. You're not going to leave it there, are you?"

"Take it off for me, O.K.? If I reach over there the board'll look like the Jolly Green Giant walked across it."

"If you're claiming the piece, take it," she said quietly.

Was she serious? Yeah, she was, damn her. "O.K.," he said. "You asked for it." He slid his arm forward. Pieces fell over and rolled. "Well, I got it off the board," he said.

One by one, Liz, patiently put all the pieces in their right places. She was taking another pawn now.

Winning, damn it. Distract her. "You going back to school," he asked.

"Oh, sure. I only took off this semester."

"Is it hard? I mean going to college—"

"In a wheelchair? Sure, it's hard."

"Do you use a motorized chair?"

"No."

"Why not?"

"I need the exercise."

Gary moved his queen. "What's it like? I mean, if you're in a chair and everybody else is—"

"Depends. There are all kinds of ABs."

"ABs?"

"Able-bodied. Some look through you as if you were invisible. Some want to know what happened to you, or"— she laughed—"they treat you as if you're retarded. And then a lot of nice people are ready to help if you ask."

"I'd feel funny asking a stranger for help."

"You'd better get used to it, if you're going to college." She moved her knight.

Gary's eyes blurred. He saw himself on a college campus begging some brawny guy to lift his chair. Ridiculous. He'd be on crutches by then. Anyhow, why would he have to ask strangers? Diane would be there. He saw clearly now that that was the only way. "What're you studying in college?" he asked.

"Science. Biology. I want to go to med school."

"Can you?"

"With my grades, if I don't get in, I'll sue."

He looked up. "Why do you want to—to knock yourself out?"

"Knock myself out? Look who's talking!"

176

That's different, he was about to say, *you've always been that way.* He caught himself.

"What I'm knocking myself out for," Liz said, "is to get into spinal-cord research."

"Yeah?" He smiled sarcastically. "You're going to find a way to fix all of us up, huh?"

"Regenerate spinal-cord tissue?" she said. "Some scientists think it'll be possible one of these days. I don't." She moved her queen. "Check," she said.

He moved his king to safety, but she closed in. "You got me," he said.

"Checkmate." She scooped up the pieces and put them in the box. "Let's play again when you're not in a trance."

"O.K. I'll beat you tomorrow night." He released the brake and pushed with his wrist cuffs on the lugs of the wheels. Liz turned off the lights and waited for him in the dimly lit corridor. "O.K., then, I'll be seeing you," he said.

She turned toward the women's wing. "Thanks for the game, and watch it tomorrow in PT," she called. "Don't knock yourself out."

"Ha." He would take her on tomorrow night, damn it, if he could only concentrate. If he could only wipe out these sexy daydreams that were driving him crazy.

Wheeling slowly past crepe-paper garlands and sprigs of evergreen, he entered the room. Tommy was plugged into his stereo. Drew and David were asleep. His turn next with the bedtime routine. The orderlies lifted him, rolled him on his side, and undressed him. He dozed for a second. What . . . ? What the hell? Treer was there—lifting his arm, at first, helping him write, and then—where were they, for Pete's sake, in her apartment?—suddenly her hands were all over him and his were all over her. . . . No, *not Treer.* Couldn't have been. Must've been Diane he was dreaming about. Now he was wide awake and the nurse was here, washing him, increasing circulation enough so that when he looked down at himself he saw an erection. Erect, but beyond his control. Pathetic, he thought, looking at himself. Now, if you were looking for an example, *there* was something that was really pathetic.

chapter **20**

"Gary, open your presents." Diane was sitting close to him with her elbows on his lapboard.

"Now?" He looked at the packages on the table.

"I want to see if you like it. I can exchange it if you don't. Right, Jason—he should open them now?"

"O.K. by me." Jason leaned against Gary's bed.

"Wait a little," Gary said.

Ann, coming back from the water fountain, waited in the hall before going back into the room. She felt edgy. The Christmas season in general maybe, or what had happened with Billy. Or the changes in Gary this week. Christmas was a rough time.

And the business with Billy had gotten things off to a

bad start. At the last minute Billy hadn't been able to come. "Guess he's got better things to do on Christmas Eve," Gary had said. Kids' friendships were always running hot and cold, Ann reminded herself. Still, try to convince Gary that Billy's fading away was just one of those things.

Ann looked in at Gary now. Tomorrow she'd be going home for a whole week—a bad time for her to leave. His behavior in the last couple of days had been erratic. John Vacaro had noticed it, too, and Gary's journal reflected it. "No matter how much you like a person who visits," he'd written, "you can't help thinking, 'Easy for you to be cheerful. You can get up and go whenever you want.' " Another day he had written, "Most people who come to see me do it because it makes *them* feel good." Gary's ups and downs were affecting her more and more, she realized.

"Don't you think you've gotten too emotionally attached to this kid?" her friend Ellen had asked this afternoon. "Yes," she had said.

She stepped into the room.

"Open them now, Gary," Diane was saying. "As soon as Ms. Treer comes back."

"I'm here," Ann said. She sat down next to Diane.

"This one's from me," Diane said. "And this is Ms. Treer's, and Jason's. Billy sent this."

"Billy's got an early acceptance," Jason said. "Ivy League —dig that."

Gary nodded. "Buck told me. Buck and Wally were here this afternoon."

"Buck's not going to retire, you know," Jason said.

"Yeah." Gary pulled Diane's gift toward him. "Can't come that close and quit, he told me."

Diane reached out. "I'll unwrap it for you, Gary."

"No, let me try." He caught the ribbon on the edge of his

wrist splint and tugged, but the ribbon held fast. He hooked his thumb in it. "Damn," he said. Then wedging the package between his upper arms, he pulled on the ribbon with his teeth.

"Gary, I'll do it!" Diane said.

He bit the ribbon in two and it fell away. "See?" he said. "I never appreciated my teeth until now. My mother keeps throwing a fit, though, at the stuff I'm putting in my mouth these days." He fixed his teeth on the wrapping paper and tore it off.

Jason watched, arms folded. "What's playing here tonight, man, *Jaws II?*

"You gotta adapt," Gary said. Placing his wrists on either side of the box top, he lifted it, but the top and bottom stuck firmly together.

Everything took so long, Ann thought. Everything became so self-conscious. Unless he's in real trouble, don't offer help, John had told her. *Sit on your hands.*

Gary jerked the box lid. "Shit!"

The three of them watched in silence. Diane reached out again. "Gary, let me open it, please?"

"I'll get it!" he said. He shook the box again, and it fell to the floor.

Jason, picking it up, loosened the lid and handed it back to him. "Wham it once more, Gary. I'd open it for you, but how else you gonna get rid of all those frustrations?"

Gary jerked the box and it opened. "Hey, that's great, Diane—Christian Dior! Do you see the shirt, Ms. Treer? Thanks a lot, Diane. I really like it."

"They had a striped one, too," she said. "Would you rather have striped?"

"No, no, this is great. Your present, the one I'm giving you, Diane, I'll give it to you later, O.K.? Jason—Ms. Treer

—I've got something for you, too. Something I wrote. I didn't—ha—I didn't get around to doing much Christmas shopping this year."

"I'm so glad you like it, Gary," Diane said. "I wasn't sure if you would." She set aside the box and held up Ann's gift for him.

He grasped it and tore at the tissue with his teeth. "Hey, nice," Gary said. "Is it for writing another journal? Nice cover."

"It's for putting whatever you like in it," Ann said.

"Thanks, Ms. Treer. Now what do we got here?" Gary pulled a brown bag toward him. "Too small for a six-pack."

"I didn't bother with none of them ribbons." Jason slouched on the bed.

"I know what it is," Diane said.

Gary turned the bag upside down and a cassette fell out. "A tape? What is it?"

"A homemade job," Jason said. *"The Wit and Wisdom of Jason Lovett.* I got some other people on there, too, friends of yours—the team. Good for a few chuckles."

"Thanks. You heard it, Diane? Did you, Ms. Treer?"

"I did," Diane said. "It's so funny—"

"No, not Ms. Treer!" Jason interrupted. "Rated X for teachers. Too many of 'em mocked out on that thing."

"Should we listen to it now?" Gary asked.

"Naw, embarrassing! Seriously, play it when you're alone, when you want to remember your buddies."

"Oh," Diane held up an envelope. "This is from Billy, Gary. Want me to—"

"Skip it," Gary said. "I'll open it later."

Diane laid the envelope on the table and picked up the wrappings from the floor. "Are your parents coming by tonight?" she asked.

"No, they were here before. They're going to church."

"Somebody's coming," Jason said.

They heard voices in the hall. "Must be Tommy," Gary said. "He was in here before feeling happy. Somebody sneaked him a bottle. He said he'd be back."

Diane leaned over and put her hand on Gary's. "He didn't give you a drink, did he?"

"I had a shot," he said. "Hell, it's Christmas." He looked at Ann. "So what? I'm hardly getting any medication. It won't hurt."

"Did your parents know you had it?" Ann asked.

"No. Hey, what is this, can't a guy celebrate Christmas? Tommy, come in here, man!" Gary called.

Tommy wheeled through the doorway. Behind him came Drew with a bottle of liquor and a stack of paper cups in his lap. Tommy closed the door.

"Drew?" Gary said. "What the hell are you doing here? I thought you left this afternoon."

Drew put his finger to his lips. "Shhh—I'm laying low," he said, pulling up to Gary. "Dr. Greenstone's coming around wishing everybody a merry. When he comes in here, hide the sauce."

"O.K., does everybody know everybody?" Gary asked.

"I believe so." Drew's speech was slurred. "Hello, Ann . . . Diane, right? And . . . Jason." Drew looked around the room. "Hey, I see I forgot my poster over the bed. A present, Gary. A present to you, O.K.? Keep it, man."

"Thanks," Gary said.

Drew swiveled his chair. "And where's the silent roommate? Did he leave?"

"David Kearns?" Gary asked. "Yeah, he left after you did this afternoon. He'll be back New Year's. When are you going for good, Drew?"

"Tonight."

"Tonight?" Gary said. "Who's coming for you, your wife? Funny, when you left this afternoon, I thought that was it. How come you came back?"

Drew smiled. "Can't bear to leave the place."

"Come on, man, you for real?" Jason asked.

"I—I had to bring Gordy and a couple of other guys a bottle," Drew said. "Couldn't break a promise to my buddies, could I?"

"How'd you get back here?" Gary asked.

"Same way as I left."

"Your wife? What time's she coming for you?"

"Late."

"Hell," Gary said, "why didn't you two just spend a quiet Christmas Eve at home?"

"Couldn't break a promise to my buddies, could I?" Drew said.

Tommy held out his cup.

"Where's your manners, Frechette?" Drew said. "Wait'll we give everybody else a drink." He poured. "Ann, a little scotch—how about it?"

"That's too much for me," she said.

Drew gave the cup to Jason and poured a shorter one.

"No, thanks, really," she insisted.

"Come on," Drew urged. "It's Christmas! We're gonna toast. We're gonna toast to everybody in this room at Phillips, the best goddam rehabilitation institute in the world. Come on, Ann!"

She took the cup reluctantly. Drew handed drinks around, set one on Gary's lapboard.

"Give the kid a straw!" Tommy said.

Drew pulled one from his shirt pocket and put it in Gary's drink. "O.K., everybody set now?" He held up his cup. "First, to Superquad, here, and his beautiful girl friend, and his beautiful teacher, and—"

"—his beautiful buddy," Jason said.

"Right on!" Drew drank and raised his cup again. "And here's to our singing group—did you hear the four of us next door—Tommy, Gordy, José, and me?"

"The Four Gimps," Tommy mumbled. "That's our name, The Four Gimps."

"And to those who aren't here—to David Kearns, our roommate, wherever he is, as he rides silently into the night on the Silver Bullet Express. . . ." Drew, his forehead damp with sweat, refilled his cup. "And—"

"And here's to you and your wife, man!" Gary said. "You're getting out of here!"

"Right," Drew said, toasting. "And here's to Cominski down the hall, who's going to sleep straight through from tonight until New Year's—"

"And here's to . . . Dr. Roth," Tommy said, draining his cup. "May Santy Claus take her into his sack for Christmas, so she'll be less of a . . ." Tommy bent over and whispered to Drew.

Gary was laughing, Ann saw, but it was forced, as if he were seeing beyond tonight to Christmas tomorrow, and next year, and all the years to come. Diane stared into her cup. Jason, reserved, stood with his arms folded.

"A little more, please," Gary said.

Diane caught Gary's eye.

"Don't *worry*, Diane. I didn't take any medication today. I can handle a couple of drinks!"

Ann got up. She had to move, to do something.

"What's the matter, Ms. Treer?" Gary asked.

"Excuse me for a minute."

"Is something wrong?" he asked.

She looked at him intently. "No," she said. She went into the hall, stood for a minute leaning against cool tiles. What the matter was, of course, she couldn't tell him. The matter was that she felt, as if it were her own, his pain—his hurt over Billy, his frustration with the Christmas wrappings, his envy of the visitors who could get up and walk out, as she had just done. She felt his anger at himself, too, for drinking when he shouldn't, and his disappointment that the drinking didn't help. The matter was that she felt all this and couldn't do anything about it, because nobody, however willing, could assume the pain of somebody else. The only thing she could do, now that she was going away, was to encourage him to write in his journal. That was still his best safety valve.

Ann heard footsteps in the corridor. Good. She'd go inside and tell them. They'd have to put the bottle away now. It was Dr. Greenstone, coming to wish them all a merry.

chapter **21**

"Happy New Year, Gary." His Aunt Evelyn squeezed his hand.

"Thanks, same to you."

She bent over his chair and kissed him on the forehead. "We'll see each other real soon. I hate to leave, to take your parents away from you like this on a holiday. I told them I'd call a cab, but—Helen?" She looked at his mother. "Does he feel warm to you?"

"I'm supposed to, Ma. I'm alive, right?" Good, they'd both gotten the message. They weren't going to stuff a thermometer in his mouth. Hell, if anything, he was chilly. Big, wet flakes of snow were falling outside.

"Keep track of the game for me, Gary," his father said. "I say USC by ten points."

"O.K." Gary shivered. A girl on TV, practically nude, was waving at them now from her rose-covered float.

"Is there anything at all we can get you before we go?" his mother asked. "I'm sorry you don't have company. I'd feel better if somebody were here."

"It's O.K.," he said. "The game's on TV. Tommy'll be back. The nurse'll be in."

"Well then, we'll say good-bye. We'd better get a head start on this snow." His mother kissed him.

"Good-bye, Gary." His aunt gave him a kiss and turned quickly away.

"Come on, girls." His father took each of them by the arm. "Happy New Year, Gary. We'll call you when we get back from the airport."

He watched them go, strained to hear if they were saying anything about him as they left. No sound except the droning voice of the TV sportscaster.

Now what . . . watch the game? Hell, he was bored with it, had been since the kickoff. He glanced down at the notebook on his lapboard, the book Treer had given him for Christmas. Write? God, no. What was the use of writing anymore, when he didn't intend for anybody to read it?

Not even Treer. The poem he'd mailed her the other day—he shouldn't have. It would probably upset her when she got it. Why drag her into this? It was his thing. All he wanted to do now was to hide the stuff he'd written. Especially the junk in his journal about why Willy Loman killed himself. Weird that the guy had done it not just because he was unhappy but because he loved his family and figured they'd be better off without him. *Nobody* was going to see that journal. He'd hide it, if he could find a good place. It'd be awful if anybody in this place got their hands on it.

Anybody in this place. He shivered again. There *wasn't* anybody in this place. The silence had been getting to him more and more each day of this last week. Halls like echo chambers. A handful of losers in the dining room. Everybody had split. Drew was home for good now. The nurse had found him in his bed at Phillips on Christmas morning. He'd been too drunk to leave the night before. His brother had had to pick him up in the afternoon—wife must've been so mad she wouldn't come back for him. David Kearns was due in this afternoon, as if that made any difference. Poor loner bastard. Liz hadn't returned yet, or Gordy or José. Just Tommy and him—Tommy down the hall, playing poker with some old geezers.

Goddamit. He was shaking like a madman now. Nervous, probably, or maybe coming down with the flu. He pressed the button for the nurse. Diane had said last night that the flu was going around. Diane was deserting him, too, today, to be with her parents. . . . Just as well, after last night. And all his other friends out of town. Jason down in Virginia for the weekend. Billy—ha! *Friend*. Nothing but a Christmas card in the last month. Treer. Treer should be back. Had she gotten his poem? Maybe she'd call. Hell, why should she? What was he to her—a crippled kid she felt sorry for?

Where was the goddam nurse? He was freezing now. He wheeled over to his bed and grabbed at the blanket on the end of it, but it slipped to the floor. Shit! He rang the nurse's bell again. He could go looking for her, but he shouldn't have to. What kind of place was this, where the staff took off on holidays and left you to rot? Maybe he

189

could get into bed by himself. He wheeled to the side of it, started to release the panel of his chair. Jesus, forget it. He could never make it. His balance was lousy. He had no transfer board and nowhere near enough strength in his arms to pull himself. He could just picture it—him falling on the floor and lying there until New Year's night. Calling for help and nobody hearing him except Tommy, who naturally wouldn't leave a poker game.

He made a futile movement toward the blanket lying on the floor. No way he could get it. Hell, give up! Get used to your station in life, man! Sit here and freeze. Get used to people keeping you waiting and then telling you how sorry they were. Aunt Evelyn . . . Jesus, he'd been annoyed as hell at her that first day she came. But when you thought about it, she was the only honest one in the bunch. She'd said out loud what they all must have been thinking the whole time—*what a terrible thing!* Hey, Aunt Evelyn, come on back. Give me the full story. Tell me how awful I look, what a burden I am! *That's* what they're thinking when they come here and smile.

The telephone was ringing. Had to be for him. Who? Too soon for his parents to call. He wheeled quickly to the phone on the post and pressed the button with the back of his hand.

"Gary Madden?" the operator asked.

"Yes."

A whirr, like a spaceship taking off. A dial tone.

"The connection seems to be cut off," the operator said. "If the party tries again, I'll ring you."

Damn it! Who was it? Worse than no call at all!

He jammed his elbow full force against the nurse's bell. "Shit!" he called as loudly as he could. He was going nuts. Shut up, man. Cool it. Wait for your phone call. Better yet, watch the football game like a good quad. Let 'em find you dead of frostbite. Let 'em be sorry. Or would they be?

He forced himself to fix his eyes on the set. Rose Bowl crowd going hysterical over a Minnie Mouse made of five million flowers. Band playing "I'm Looking Over a Four-Leaf Clover." *Happy New Year!* If one more person said those words to him today, he was going to—do what? *Do what?* What a jerk he was. What could he do that mattered? About the best he could manage was *not* to do something, like back at St. Agnes, when he'd refused to eat. A pathetic game. Everything was striking him that way. It was getting clearer and clearer that he had no power, except maybe the power to say no, the power *not* to do things. Real power belonged to ABs—to those jocks there, running onto the field after half time, to Billy and Jason who'd be joining them soon, to Diane, who eventually would have had it with him and would choose making it with an AB instead of lying, like last night, on a hospital bed with somebody who couldn't feel.

He pressed the TV remote-control button. There—wipe 'em out. Waste 'em. The screen went black except for a tiny lingering white dot. A creaking inside the wall, a far-away clunk emphasized the quiet of the room. The stillness hypnotized him. He pressed the button again, waited until the players appeared in kickoff formation for the pleasure of clearing the screen once more. Zap. Down the drain. See? That was as far as his power went, sitting here pressing buttons, sitting here shivering and pretending stuff, while they were out there, for real, running and passing and tackling and fucking under the California sun. *Living.* While he . . . lousy, fuckin' luck. Why him? *Why him?* What had *he* done?

"Sorry, Gary, I heard your bell but I was tied up with Mr. Filippi. What can I do for you?"

The nurse—it was the nurse Maureen—standing in the doorway. Sorry, naturally. "I need a blanket or a sweater," Gary said. Suddenly he felt hot.

Maureen came over to him and felt his forehead. She picked up the blanket from the floor and put it around his shoulders. "Let's check your temperature. You don't feel good, do you?"

"No—weak."

"Want to get into bed? I'll get help. Here, meanwhile put this under your tongue, O.K.? I'll be right back. Good, here comes company for you. Tommy, don't let him talk with the thermometer in his mouth."

Maureen left and Tommy wheeled in. "Hey, man, you sick?"

Gary shrugged his shoulders.

Tommy backed up. "Don't give *me* nothing." He pulled out a pack of cigarettes and lit up. "I just lost my shirt. Thirty-five bucks to Pop Johnson, the dude with one leg. He's gotta be in the black Mafia, that guy. Hey, buddy, I just heard something bad. *Overheard* something, that is." Tommy wheeled closer. "I've heard some rotten stuff in my day, but this beats all." He took a drag, let out smoke slowly through his nose. "I know you don't dig my stories, but this is about somebody you *know*. You'll hear it sooner or later, buddy, better from me. . . ."

Gary, trapped with the thermometer, said nothing.

Tommy knocked an ash onto the floor. "I'm not supposed to know this, by the way. I just happened to have heard it. Enough people know already, so there's no stopping it. Otherwise I'd keep my mouth shut. You know Christmas Eve, when Drew came back with the booze?"

Gary nodded.

"You know why Drew came back Christmas Eve and got smashed and stayed overnight?"

Gary shook his head. He was shaking now with chills. His eyes were burning.

Tommy dragged on his cigarette. "It was his brother came when he got discharged and drove him home in the afternoon. They say Drew got out of the car and walked into his house on crutches and found the place half cleaned out."

Robbed? Gary looked up.

"Cleaned out," Tommy repeated. "His wife had took half their stuff and walked out on him. Just like that." Tommy snapped his fingers. "Left a note saying she was sorry, but she'd been thinking about it and she didn't see how it could work between them anymore."

Gary's teeth came down hard on the thermometer. At first he thought he'd bitten it in half. He spit it out onto the floor.

"What're you doing, man? Hey, how do you like that—it didn't break!"

Gary's tongue felt thick, his mouth bitter, as if mercury really had escaped. "She went—*for good?*" he asked.

"Gone with the wind—and do you know what kills me?" Tommy inhaling deeply. "Drew knew it all the time he was here Christmas Eve, when he was joking around and toasting and all that crap, and he *never said one word*. That cool sonofabitch never said one word, played it like he was happy to come back and get a load on with his buddies. Even Christmas Day when he left, he was pinching nurses' fannies. *He never let on.* How's that for guts?"

"I thought—he was always talking about her—said she was so . . . You met her, Tommy, how the hell could she . . . ?" Gary felt the sweat dripping from his armpits.

"Some are angels, buddy, and some are whores. I guess he figured her wrong. Hey, Maureen." Tommy pointed to the floor. "Gary lost something."

"How'd you do that, Gary?" Maureen picked up the thermometer. "It's not broken. Did you have it under your tongue long enough?"

"Yeah. What does it read?" Gary asked.

She examined it. "Into bed," she said. "You've got a temperature of 103. I'll get help and we'll put you in bed fast. I sent word to Dr. Roth that you're not feeling good. She'll probably want to take an X-ray and send a urine sample downstairs."

Gary closed his eyes. His head was pounding. "What do you think it is?"

"The X-ray'll show if you've got a respiratory infection," Maureen said, "and the urinalysis will show if it's your bladder. You'll be O.K., Gary, don't worry. Here's the aide. Come on, let's get you comfortable."

Feeling foggy now, as if the snow outside were swirling in front of his eyes. They were wheeling him, lifting, bearing him up like a corpse. Maureen taking off his shirt, like Diane had done last night. Diane had started out fine, rubbing his shoulders. All he'd wanted was to have her lying there next to him. Afraid of hurting him, she'd said. Afraid of bumping his neck brace. Don't worry, he'd told her, but she had worried all the same, and so had he. "We've got plenty of time," Diane had said. "We'll get used to things." Sure, sure. Had Drew's wife said that, too?

"Where is he?" Gary asked.

"Who?" Maureen was putting his arm in the pajama sleeve.

Her fingers felt icy against his shoulder. He was on fire now. "Where's Drew?" he called. "Hey, Tommy, where's Drew? What's he doing about it? Tommy? Where is he?"

"He's O.K.," Tommy said from far away across the room. "He's home with his brother. He's O.K."

Gary heard a humming in his ears. The fever? Respiratory infection, she'd said. He'd heard of quads dying from that. Or maybe bladder infection. Kimball had warned him —urine could back up, stones could form. Hey, Kimball, I drank my cranberry juice, swear I did. They say that cleans you out. Why didn't it? Why *me*, Kimball—Roth? Buck, why me? I wasn't too tense, Buck, just up for the game. Why me, Lionetti? I didn't tackle too high, man—the films proved it!

Blankets piled on him now. Forget it, Maureen, I'm hot! A new voice, Dr. Roth's. Shoving a thermometer in his mouth again. Eyes closed, faces floating . . . Diane's . . . Drew's wife's. . . . The murmuring of Roth's voice.

Suddenly he knew exactly how it was going to be. He was going to die. They'd knock themselves out first, naturally. They'd call people—specialists, his parents, Diane, his friends. They'd call Treer, and at the very end, Pastor Shafer. They'd do everything they could, but he was going to die anyway. And they would lower him into the ground and the snow would cover up the new grave, and they would all walk away from the cemetery together and . . . it would be an enormous relief to everyone.

And the biggest relief of all would be to him. Because then nobody'd have to see him helpless anymore or worry about him or feel guilty about leaving him. And if it happened like this—an infection—it would be natural, much better than Willie Loman's fake car accident. Just a quad croaking from a respiratory infection. Simple as that. *God took him*, Shafer would say, and they'd all be heartbroken, but they'd accept it, and deep down *they'd be relieved.*

What was Roth doing now? Poking in his mouth, taking out the thermometer. How high, Roth? Won't tell? *You'll be O.K., Gary*, Maureen had said. Maybe she could sucker some patients, not him. He was going to die. Unless—what if this thing didn't kill him, just left him weaker, more helpless, like David Kearns? Never—never—he swore.

Suddenly it came clear to him, so *clear*, out of the cloud inside his head! The best way to pull off his act of love. He'd almost done it before by accident—so easy! Bite the thermometer, really hard. Swallow the jagged particles of glass, the dense little silver ball that would split apart inside him and split again and again until pinheads of silver filled his bloodstream. They'd miss the thermometer—pump stomach—operate—too late. Don't tell my mother how, he'd beg with his last breath. Jesus, perfect. He'd do it. When they took his temperature *next time.*

"Hey Tom!" he called. His own voice sounded cheerful to him now. He was happy, like Willy Loman!

"Your medication's here, Gary," Maureen was saying. "Open your mouth. That's it. Swallow. Now—sleep, Gary."

Couldn't sleep. Had to know first. On his mind all this time. "Tommy! Hey, Tommy . . . buddy . . ." Room spinning—a blizzard in his head.

"Yeah?"

"That quad—the one in the breath-powered wheelchair. The one with the good-looking wife—"

"What the hell're you talking about?"

"The quad who went home weekends, until one time—you know, the guy you told me about at St. Agnes, when I asked you to shut up."

"Yeah?"

"What happened to him? What finally happened to him, Tommy?"

"Nothing, man."

"Screw you, Tommy! *What happened to him?*" He was mad now, hot and cold at the same time, and carrying this heavy bundle, like in his old dream. "Tell me, Tommy! I want to *know.*"

"He lived happily ever after."

"The hell he did!" Gary shouted. Sweat was in his eyes. The blankets were suffocating him. "I know what happened —he wasted himself, didn't he? I knew it! Down the drain, *right*, Tommy?"

chapter **22**

"You're his teacher—a friend of the family, aren't you? I've seen you here." Dr. Roth stood outside the door of Gary's room.

"Yes, I'm Ann Treer. Is anything wrong?"

Dr. Roth reached in the pocket of her white coat and took out a slip of paper. "I've been trying to call the Maddens," she said. "Gary's on the sick list. He's got a bladder infection."

"Is it serious?"

"No, but I'm anxious to explain to them before they call and find out from someone else. We've had a lot of confusion around here this evening."

"May he have visitors? I usually call before I come, but

I just got back from a week out of town. I've been concerned, so I came over on the spur of the moment."

"You may see him," Dr. Roth said. "He was out of it for a while there, but we've gotten his temperature down in the last hour."

"You say it's not serious?"

They moved away from the door. "No," Dr. Roth said, "it's almost routine with spinal-cord patients. It's no joke— he feels miserable. But we've started him on antibiotics. He'll be better in a week or so." She paused. "That's not our main concern now, though."

"No?"

Dr. Roth folded and unfolded the paper in her hand. "We've had—we learned something very sad this evening about one of our patients. We try to keep this sort of thing confidential, but there's been a news leak already. I don't know for sure, but I'm afraid Gary may have heard about it. You ought to know the facts if you're going to see him. You can help us, actually, by keeping him company until his family arrives."

"I'll do anything I can," Ann said.

Dr. Roth shielded her eyes with her hand. "This is only the second case in my experience—it's a rare thing, really. I'm sorry if I'm not being very clear. Had you met David Kearns, the young man who was in with Gary?"

"Yes."

"David left here over a week ago for the holidays. He was supposed to have come back today. This evening we got word of his death. He committed suicide at home."

Ann pressed her fingertips together and looked at the floor.

"Nineteen years old," Dr. Roth said. "If you saw David, you know that he was withdrawn, but—well, we felt before he left for the vacation that we were finally making a little progress. And then this."

"I think it'll hit Gary hard if he knows."

"The timing couldn't be worse," Dr. Roth said, "with his sickness and on top of . . . It's been a hellish week around here. The worst in my memory. Everybody's morale's been affected by what happened to Drew. Drew Hutchins, Gary's other roommate who was discharged. His wife left him."

"I didn't know," Ann said.

Dr. Roth shrugged. "At least, if anybody can shake a thing like that, Drew can. We've been in touch with him, and he's O.K. But *this week* and *this room*. It kind of makes you worry that you're jinxed. That's why I'm keeping a check. John Vacaro tells me you're close to Gary. To your knowledge, has he been depressed?"

"Yes. It's come out mostly in his writing," Ann said. "He wrote a poem that I have with me. Frankly, I'm concerned. His girl friend's upset, too. She called me this afternoon and sent a note along for him. That's one reason I came over this evening."

"Perhaps you'd be willing to talk to John Vacaro for a minute when he comes."

Ann studied the wedge of yellow light coming from Gary's room. "I'll do whatever will help."

"Do you want to see Gary now?" Dr. Roth asked. "He's by himself. We'll appreciate it if you can keep him company until his parents come."

"I'll do my best."

"Good. I'm going to try calling his parents again. I'll be back as soon as I can."

Ann went to the door of his room. Two beds were vacant, table and bureau tops bare—Drew's and David's. She glanced at the poster still taped over Drew's old bed, the poster he'd left behind that read, "If life gives you lemons, make lemonade." Tommy wasn't around. Gary lay on his back, awake, a sheet drawn up to his neck brace. She walked toward the bed. "Gary? Hi."

He tried to turn, to focus his eyes. Perspiration glistened on his forehead.

"Hi, Gary."

"Hey . . ." He breathed heavily, tried to cough. "Thought I was dreaming . . . Tea Runner . . . did they send for you? My parents here? Shafer?"

"No," she said, "just me." She came closer to the bed. "Dr. Roth's trying to call your parents. They'll be over, probably."

"You came by yourself?"

"Yes. Diane's parents wouldn't let her, in the snowstorm. She wanted to. I brought a note from her."

"Diane?" He tried to raise himself. "I thought I heard my mother talking. And Shafer. I'm so hot. I'm talking like a dope, aren't I? Anybody else here?"

Ann took off her coat. "Just me, Gary. Keep lying down. Are you too tired to talk?"

"No, no I want to."

"Well, then, lie back. Here, do you want to see the message from Diane?"

He blinked in confusion. "Yeah. Read it to me, O.K.?"

She took it out of her bag. "It's dated this afternoon, four o'clock. It says, 'Dear Gary, I tried to call you, but I couldn't get through. What happened last night doesn't matter. We have so much that's good—let's save it. There's lots of time. I'm feeling so bad, and only you can help me. Love, as ever, Diane.'"

Gary twisted his neck in the brace. "She brought it to

your house? The note? They wouldn't let her come? Let's see her handwriting, Ms. Treer, please."

Ann held it up.

He squinted. "Can't see straight," he said. "Wish I could *see*. See *her*. Tell her thanks, Ms. Treer. You the only one here? My parents? Where's the nurse? When are they going to take my temperature?"

"I don't know."

He licked his lips. "Tell them to take it now."

Ann laid the note from Diane on his table. "The nurse isn't here, Gary. Dr. Roth said she'll be back soon. I'll ask her when she comes. You know what's wrong with you, don't you? You know it's a bladder infection and you'll be all right in a few days, as soon as the antibiotic works? Did Dr. Roth explain that?"

Gary blinked. "She told you that, too?"

"Yes."

"And you believed it?"

"Sure, why not?"

Gary looked at her intently. "With us—*the truth*, right?"

"We've managed that, I think, yes."

"I trust you, but not the others."

"Why, do you think Dr. Roth has lied to you?"

He lay very still. "Yes," he whispered. "I can't *see*, except stuff inside my head. Wild stuff. I can't think right. I'm burning up."

She touched his hand. "You've had fever before. That's the way it is with a fever. For everybody. Last time I had the flu, I wanted to die, and then as quickly as it came the fever went and I was on the mend. Let me get you a drink, O.K.?" She poured water, held the straw, remembered the first time she had given him a drink at St. Agnes.

He sipped. "Fever wrecks your brain," he said.

"It's under control," she said. "Dr. Roth says it's not serious. You're going to start feeling better soon."

Water trickled out of the corner of his mouth. "If you knew I was going to die," he whispered, "would you tell me?"

She took out a tissue and wiped away the water on his lips. "That would depend on a lot of things."

"No copping out—the truth!"

"The truth is, I'm not sure." She put the tissue on the table. "I'd do whatever I thought would help you the most. I don't think I could lie to you. And there's no reason to. A doctor I trust says you'll be well in a week. That's the truth as I know it."

"Swear?"

"I swear."

He was silent for a minute. "Let's say I get better this time, and then the same thing happens again and again—that's how it goes, I hear."

"They try to track down the cause."

"And if they can't fix it?"

"They keep trying."

"Ms. Treer," he said, "ask the nurse to take my temperature, please."

Ann felt his forehead. Perspiration moistened her palm. "Gary, the fever's already broken. You're going to start feeling better. I swear."

"Have her take it with the thermometer!"

"When she comes, Gary."

"Now!"

Ann sat on the edge of the bed. "Why?"

"To finish it, to get it over with."

"Finish? Finish what?"

"Finish everything. Be done with it. *Leave.*"

"Leave the people you love, like in your poem?"

"Yes."

"What does the thermometer have to do with it?"

He clamped his teeth together and swallowed. "Mercury, glass. Neat—huh, Ms. Treer? I wasn't going to tell you, but— you I can trust, right? David Kearns found a way. Didn't think he had the guts." He laughed giddily. "Down the drain, Ms. Treer. Nurses talking about it when they thought I was dozing. Gotta tell Tommy. Oh, boy, heard some gross stuff going down in my day, but this beats all! Hey, Tommy, wherever you are—this quad, David Kearns, was in this private house that his parents built for him, and the nurse— shouldn't have—the nurse left him alone, and there was this filled bathtub, and he released the panel of his chair and let himself down—down the drain!"

Ann put her hand on his. "What David Kearns did has nothing to do with you. You know that, don't you?"

He looked up, dazed. "And Drew—did you hear about Drew? Drew went in his house and found the place half cleaned out—she walked out on him for good."

"That has nothing to do with you, either. Gary . . ."

He smiled and shivered. "Ms. Treer, can you not want something and want it at the same time?"

"I'm not sure. What?"

"To die."

"I felt like that when I had the flu, Gary. And then you get better and the whole world looks different."

"But I wanted to die before I got sick—yesterday and the day before that."

"I've felt that, too. Do you believe me? I've felt that, too. And finally it starts to go away."

"I wanted to die when I wrote the poem. You have the poem with you?"

"Yes."

She fumbled in her bag and looked at the looseleaf page again.

Leaving

I am the weight
I dream about!
I rest upon the shoulders
of the ones I love;
I exert my power,
bear down,
break away,
leaving them
to walk
unburdened.

"What do you think of it, Ms. Treer? As a poem?

"It's honest. I like the way the lines break—it does what poems are supposed to do."

"What?"

"It makes me feel."

"I felt like dying when I wrote it. David Kearns had guts."

"No."

"What's the point, Ms. Treer, when you're trapped in a chair?"

"It's got wheels."

"Sure, you can go some places, do some things, but it's not the same. Everything's second-rate."

"Your mind isn't second-rate. It's untouched. Sharper than before the accident. You can see and hear and smell and talk. You have memories and you can work out prob-

lems and you have emotions. That's enough for a full life."
She was burning too, now, as if the fever were contagious.

Gary shook his head. "Half a life," he said, breathing quickly. "Would you call me a coward if I did what David did?"

She didn't answer.

"How could you? It would be like Willy, Willy Loman. An act of love."

"That's what *he* thought, but Willy was wrongheaded." She felt the heat rising faster. "Willy miscalculated. He thought he was helping his family, but were they better off? Did they respect him for doing it?"

"No."

"Did his wife miss him and need him?"

"Yeah, him, maybe. What does that have to do with me?"

"You don't think anybody needs *you?*" she said. "What about your parents?"

"Easier without me."

"Since when do your parents value their ease?"

He was silent.

"Diane says she needs you," Ann said, "in that note."

"She's putting me on."

"You don't trust Diane?"

"I believe she means it now, but—"

"Isn't *now* where we are?"

He breathed out painfully. "I can't help looking ahead."

"Well then, look to college, to meeting other girls if it doesn't work out with Diane, to getting a job, to setting an example for other people—like John Vacaro's done, for instance."

"I'm not John."

"I know. You're not Drew, either, or David Kearns, who

died the way he lived—a shadow. And you're certainly not Willy Loman, a wornout man who spent his whole life avoiding the truth. You're not like them, but you can learn something from them. Drew's down, but he's not beaten. He's doing O.K. Dr. Roth says so. And most of all, you can learn something from John. He's been exactly where you are. He could help you if you let him."

Gary cleared his throat. "Listen, Ms. Treer, thanks for trying, but forget it, please. I'm beat. Some people want to lose, remember? You said it once. I'm beat. No endurance. Wish I had it, like in your metaphor—swimming with grace and ease and all that. What's mine? What's my metaphor, Ms. Treer? I never found one. A weight sinking . . . in a bathtub? How's that? A blob of mercury splitting . . . an atom? Get the nurse, Ms. Treer, tell her to *bring the thermometer*."

"No, I won't." Her voice broke. She bent over him. "Gary, listen, the thermometer won't do what you want it to. And if it could, do you think I'd sit here and let you try it?" She felt her eyes filling up. "I'm not going to let you leave. I'm one of the people who needs you—a lot."

He looked at her. "What for?"

"To make me feel." She paused. "For a while I've been afraid I couldn't anymore. You taught me I could."

"What did I do?"

"Talked, tried hard at everything, trusted me, joked, played games. Were . . . yourself."

"I'm not myself anymore."

"Whatever self you've been showing me, it's a great self. Your family, your old friends, they knew the Gary you think is lost. But I didn't know you before the accident. Not really. All I know is you in your new life. You may think you can't do much, but I'm proof that you can make people feel, make people need you *now*." She wiped her face with the back of her hand.

Gary stared.

Ann covered her eyes, put her head down, and laid her face against the sheet.

"Ms. Treer? Hey, Ms. Treer . . . please." He shifted so that he touched her hair with his shoulder.

She cried freely, quietly, an outpouring that brought her, gradually, relief. The tears soaked into the sheet. She wondered if he felt them. Then, her own quivering letting up, she listened to his labored breathing. At last she sat and looked at him, her vision foggy. "Sorry," she said, reaching for a tissue. "I'm all right now. I guess I did that because I've been trying *not* to for so long."

He didn't answer, and when she wiped her eyes, she saw that his, too, were brimming.

"I didn't mean to hurt you," he said in a husky voice.

"I know. You don't have to say anything. I know."

He blinked, and when the tears spilled over he made no attempt to stop them. They looked at each other in silence, and her own eyes filled again.

"Buck and Wally should see me now," he whispered, closing his eyes. "Don't tell."

"Never," she said. "Our deepest secret."

"Hey, don't tell anybody about the thermometer, either. O.K.?"

She nodded.

"I can picture it, in the papers," he said, half smiling, "*New Bridge Jock Croaks; Missing Thermometer Sought.*"

They exchanged a look, and both laughed. Then, burying her face in the same damp place on the sheet, her shoulders touching his, Ann laughed again. She could feel, off and on, the shaking of his shoulders as he laughed, too.

"Well," she said, finally sitting up, "I don't know about you, but I feel a little better." She wiped her eyes again, and then she wiped his face. "So don't leave, O.K.?"

"I guess I'm not going anywhere," he said. "I probably wouldn't have told you about the thermometer if I was really going to do it. What about you?" he asked suddenly. "When the tutoring's over, I mean at the end of school, then you'll be the one to leave."

"Why should I?"

"You'll keep visiting?"

"Sure."

"We'll be friends?"

"Why not? Better than most, probably. With fewer hangups than between a parent and kid, and less possessiveness than between boy friend and girl friend. Friends who play anagrams and send poems."

"I'm no poet."

"You could be, in your new life."

He shook his head. "Naa, corny, Ms. Treer—*Quad Jock Turns Poet*. Buck and Wally wouldn't dig it."

"Not so corny. Just switching from one game to another, that's all."

"Poetry's a game?"

"Sure, you make up your own rules and follow them."

"Yeah, I see what you mean—poetry, anagrams . . . both games."

"Speaking of anagrams," Ann said, "ever since you came up with DAMN RAGGEDY I've been trying for one that suits you better, but I don't think I can get one out of those letters. I guess it's impossible. We'll live with DAMN RAGGEDY and play a different game. Got to know when to quit, right?"

"Yeah," Gary said, "*Hey, wait a minute*. . . . How's

this . . . ? *Anagrams.* Anagrams as the metaphor for my life—making something new out of all the scrambled-up parts."

"Not bad," she said. "I thought you'd find one."

"How are we doing?" Dr. Roth stood in the doorway.

Ann turned around, surprised. "We're . . . O.K.," she said.

"I reached your parents, Gary," Dr. Roth called. "They're on their way. You have another visitor. He's out here in the hall talking to Tommy. A young man says his name is Jason."

"Jason's here?"

"Are you feeling well enough?" she asked.

"Yeah. Yeah, I am."

"Maureen's coming to take your temperature again. I'll be back to check it." Dr. Roth glanced at Ann. "John Vacaro's here."

"I'm going to go, Gary." Ann stood up. "Is everything O.K.?"

"Yeah. Don't worry about the thermometer, Ms. Treer. Honest."

"I won't," she said, squeezing his hand. "It's not your style. Do you have messages for anybody?"

"Tell Diane hi. Tell her thanks for the note. I was so dopey before, when you read it to me. I feel better now. Tell her I'll write. And—could you take my journal? Keep it for me? It's on the lapboard. Keep it—you know—under wraps. Some pretty heavy stuff in there."

"I'll take good care of it. Is it all right if I show the poem to John?"

Gary hesitated. "Yeah. O.K. Tell him I was just playing games."

"Keep playing them, O.K.?" she said softly. "I'll call you tomorrow."

"So long, Ms. Treer."

"So long."

Ann, picking up her things, waved to him, and went into the corridor.

"Hi, Ms. Treer, Happy New Year," Jason said. He was sitting in Tommy's wheelchair. Tommy in leg braces, stood beside him.

"Thanks, Jason, same to you. Hi, Tommy."

"Hi."

"I've just been copping a ride from this bum," Jason said. "O.K. for us to go in there now?"

"Yes," Ann nodded. "Dr. Roth says it's all right."

"Hey, Ms. Treer . . ." Jason wheeled toward her. "I hear he's sick. What's the matter? Is he feeling down?"

Ann tucked the journal under her arm. "He was," she said, turning to go. "He was, but I think he's on his way up. Go on in, Jason. He'll be glad to see you."

Robin Fidler Brancato grew up in Wyomissing, Pennsylvania, a suburban town which provided inspiration for the setting of her first novel, *Don't Sit Under the Apple Tree*. Her second novel for young people, *Something Left to Lose*, was published in 1976.

Ms. Brancato earned a B.A. in creative writing from the University of Pennsylvania and received her M.A. from the City College of New York. For the past ten years, she has taught high school English and journalism in Hackensack, New Jersey. She lives in Teaneck, New Jersey, with her husband, John, and their two sons, Christopher and Gregory.

DATE DUE